Critical Praise for Edgar Award Finalist
Havana Lunar by Robert Arellano

"Dr. Mano Rodriguez is caught up in intrigue in this thoughtful, lushly detailed neo-noir . . . Much Spanish dialogue, with prompts in English on more difficult words, deepens the sense of locale." —*Publishers Weekly*

"A sad, surreal, beautiful tour of the hell that was Cuba in the immediate aftermath of the collapse of the Soviet Union. The writing is hypnotic, the storytelling superb. *Havana Lunar* is perfect."
—Tim McLoughlin, author of *Heart of the Old Country*, editor of *Brooklyn Noir*

"Arellano engages the reader immediately by quickly developing his characters into unique individuals, both good and bad . . . *Havana Lunar* is not bashful in its presentation of Cuba and its seamy side: Arellano is savvy and able to show caring families while also introducing the reader to the grittier side . . . The detail is impressive . . . Arellano is masterful, weaving both the physical and emotional into a story everyone can relate to in some way . . ."
—*Multicultural Review*

"Written with passion and vision and with a clear, unflinching eye, Robert Arellano's *Havana Lunar* breaks new ground. It is not a Cuban American novel but a Cuban novel written in English. In it the Cuban underworld of chulos and jineteras is revealed and the über-world of political bosses and apparatchiks unmasked. I am certain that *Havana Lunar* will find a wide and enthusiastic readership."
—Pablo Medina, author of *The Cigar Roller*

"A noir novel short enough to read on a two-hour airplane ride and sufficiently satisfying to make you feel glad you read it." —*Albuquerque Journal*

"What a delight, after reading a string of uninvolving novels, to come across Robert Arellano's engaging 'Cuban noir novel,' *Havana Lunar*. The Havana setting breathes life into this story of grisly murder and false accusation . . . *Havana Lunar* has lots to enjoy, everything a comic noir aficionado could hope for." —Michael Sedano, La Bloga

"Robert Arellano's book is a hypnotic trip into another world, a place we are hardly ever allowed to go—Castro's Cuba. Without polarizing political pontifications or moral insertions of right and wrong, Arellano takes us straight into a country where people survive, combining resilience with ingenuity to keep the best of what works while simply sneaking around the things that don't. It's the way of life for most people who live under dictatorships—and yet the joy and beauty of this novel is how effortlessly he weaves his characters into our lives . . . It's as if Balzac meets Philip K. Dick, for Arellano's Cuba is a whole other planet to us, one we definitely need to know more about . . ."
—Abraham Rodriguez, author of *South by South Bronx*

"In Havana, despite the fall of the Soviet Union, a continued United States embargo, shortages of just about everything except labor, and a zeal to make do with resources at hand, life is also lived with great passion. It is that passion which suffuses Arellano's latest book, a 'Cuban noir' crime novel titled *Havana Lunar*." —*Taos News*

"The overarching rhythm of the chapters incorporates the underlying rhythm of the sentences . . . Alternating scenes, dialogue, and action create a cinematic experience . . . The intimate character of the tale has the quality of a memoir . . . a story as convincing as it is refreshing." —*Taos Horse Fly*

CURSE THE NAMES

CURSE THE NAMES

A NOVEL BY
ROBERT ARELLANO

Published by Akashic Books
©2012 Robert Arellano

ISBN-13: 978-1-61775-030-4
Library of Congress Control Number: 2011923107

Akashic Books
PO Box 1456
New York, NY 10009
info@akashicbooks.com
www.akashicbooks.com

For Donna and Dave Marston

Acknowledgments

Special thanks to Ibrahim Ahmad, Johanna Ingalls, K. Silem Mohammad, and Johnny Temple for their inspiration and advice.

This was life.
The luckiest hours
Like scribbles in chalk
On a slate in a classroom.
We stare
And try to understand them.
Then luck turns its back—
and everything's wiped out.

—Aeschylus, *The Orestia*

The time will come when mankind will curse the names of Los Alamos and Hiroshima.

—J. Robert Oppenheimer

She took my wrist in her hands and placed it on the padded, tissue-papered armrest. "Keep your elbow real straight for me now." She was what you might call a goth: black scrubs, pierced tongue, and an extreme manicure, black-polished fingernails at least three inches long. How can someone who draws blood for a living have such long nails?

There were tattoos up her inner arm: figures, faces, and names. I don't know, guys she had been with? There were girls' names too. I watched her preparations.

She tied the latex strap around my bicep and gave me a rubber ball to squeeze. Somehow she pulled a pair of surgical gloves over those nails, and then she scrubbed the crook of my arm with an alcohol swab, finding a vein she liked. I tilted my head back and closed my eyes. She jabbed the needle in and I groaned softly.

"You're lucky you have such low blood pressure," she said, and we both waited for the vial to fill. "So, what are you doing for the Fourth?"

Fourth of July: a special day for me—like the song says, "Born on."

"Staying home, probably. Fireworks make my dog skittish."

What made me say *probably* just then? And what made me refer to Oppie as just *my* dog? The same impulse that makes me take off my wedding band before entering the clinic: a just-in-case. Never mention the wife just in case you run into a woman who might want to make a pass at you.

The blood tech was holding her breath, and for the first time in our short history of brief encounters I noticed that she looked into my eyes with a strange earnestness. Back in college, that expression would have made me put down my beer at a party and follow her up the stairs no matter how she looked. I said, "What about you?"

She exhaled and flicked the strap away. A little grin stole over her usually dour pout. "Me and my girlfriends go to Morphy Lake. Have you ever been up there?"

"Is that the one near Mora?"

"Yeah. There's an abandoned house above the lake. It's the only place in that valley, right after the bend in the old road. Me and my girlfriends bring a bottle of Crown Royal and make up ghost stories." And then she said, "You should come."

"What?"

She backed out the needle and pressed a gauze pad against my skin. "You should come, we could hook up."

Hook up, that's the phrase young people use for sex, right?

For as long as things have been cooling with Kitty, I have been waiting for this to happen: a loose girl—a young woman, the likes of whose suppleness I haven't experienced since grad school—makes the first move. I am a lecher, but I am also a coward, so I have always left it up to someone else to propose an extramarital affair.

The nails got in the way and she fumbled with the Band-Aid. I had to help her put it on my arm, our fingers briefly touching. I let go of the rubber ball and she finished her job with a bit of surgical tape. I liked the way she held my wrist and gently bent my arm back at the elbow instead of saying okay, you don't have to keep it straight anymore. I liked the homemade signs she taped to all the cabinets, little penciled messages that read: *don't 4get servecing code!* and *remenber: just a little pinch!* I decided she might just be trying to pick me up. Hook up.

I took a mental picture of her ass inside those scrubs. I wanted to know what it would feel like for those long fingernails to scratch my back, draw a line of blood. In my head, I was already winding across the mountains in the Spider, and Kitty was better than a thousand miles away—even though she would be right beside me—because my mind was on a sexy young blood tech I pictured disrobing inside an abandoned house at the end of the trail. I realized I had not felt this way in fifteen years, when driving three hours to get laid was almost as good as getting laid. It simultaneously inflamed my lust and awakened an affinity for deception.

In the clinic parking lot, I climbed in the Spider, took the New Mexico map out of the glove compartment, and drew a line across the mountains.

Dozens of families went camping at Morphy Lake for Independence Day weekend, and every one of them had to drive over that awful road. Even SUVs bottomed out on the ruts, but I'm the only one who tried it in an Alfa Romeo Spider, bashing the tailpipe all to hell. Kitty and I weren't getting along, Oppie had indigestion, I stabbed myself in the hand with a tent stake, and the cap on the Dewar's somehow got open and spilled whiskey all over the trunk of the Spider. Kitty caught me trying to suck whatever I could out of the floor mat. Not an auspicious start.

Kitty said, "Are you going to give Oppie his suppository or not?"

"I gave it to him last time."

"No. I gave him the last *two* times."

"I cut my hand. I don't want to get it infected."

"Shit. How the fuck did you do that?"

"Fucking tent stake."

"You clumsy fuck."

Kitty and I shared a carefree swearing habit, the mark of a childless couple. Sometime after the tenth wedding anniversary, living in close quarters without kids to keep us in line, we embraced expletives with gusto. It rattled anyone who hung around us. We never hit each other, but people picked up on the vibe of verbal abuse, and we had no real friends. There was Dr.

and Mrs. Henry Farmer, but I can't be sure they really count. It would be more accurate to call Hank Farmer a drinking buddy, while our wives relied on each other to bicker to about their husbands' drinking.

At sunset we were eaten by mosquitoes. I had forgotten to bring the repellent.

Fire danger was just moderate, so the park rangers cleared the campground area for sparklers and small poppers only, but at dusk someone across the lake blasted "The Star-Spangled Banner" from an RV, and on cue a bunch of kids lit off some big ones on the beach: *The bombs bursting in air . . .*

The pyrotechnicians scattered before the campground host could maneuver his Bronco II around the ring road at five miles per hour.

Kitty and I watched it all from a rock while eating cold beans out of the can. The Coleman bottle I had brought didn't have anything in it.

"You stupid fuck. Couldn't you feel it was empty?"

"At least I remembered the fucking can opener."

Oppie started whimpering, so Kitty and I let up and laid our sleeping bags out in the tent. I popped the trunk of the Spider and soaked a tissue with whiskey from the floor mat as antiseptic, wrapping it around my injured hand and securing it with duct tape.

When I got in the tent Kitty was deep in her sleeping bag with her shoulder to me. I climbed into my bag still wearing a shirt, pants, and socks. I waited fifteen minutes until Kitty's breathing slowed and became shallow. I shook her shoulder to no effect. She hadn't forgotten to pack her Ambien.

I squirmed out of the sleeping bag and slipped into

my windbreaker, patting the pockets to make sure the camera and the Altoids tin were there.

Oppie, curled in a little ball at the foot of Kitty's bag, looked up and wagged his tail. I made easy-boy gestures and clipped the leash to his travel collar. If I didn't take Oppie he would whine and wake Kitty.

I unzipped the tent flap and stepped outside into my shoes.

The dark campground was quiet, the only sounds the crickets, my footfall through the brush, and the tinkling of Oppie's tags. We followed an unmarked trail out the back of the overflow parking lot. I took Oppie's leash off and we labored up the steep slope from the lake. The chirping of the crickets became louder.

What starlight made it through the trees kept us on a footpath that ended at a wire fence about a quarter-mile into the woods. I spent a minute feeling my way around the edge of the forest. Behind the broken branch of a ponderosa pine I found the cattle gate. I went over and Oppie went under.

I flicked the lighter beneath a sign nailed high to the side of a tall aspen: *Aplanado*. Sucking the makeshift bandage on my hand for a taste of the scotch, I dug in my pocket for the Altoids tin, took out a joint, and lit it.

It was a narrow dirt road, packed earth winding potholed between ancient trees. It had been here before horses and wagons. It had been here before the original Indian trail, when barefoot traders and skin-shod scouts beat the prairie grass to dust. It had been here before deer and elk carved the contours of a trail for its proximity to water. It went from nowhere to nowhere.

I smoked and walked between the ruts while Oppie

sniffed around the overgrowth at the edges. The road humped at a spot where a culvert had been installed to allow an irrigation ditch to cross under. Water trickled through the metal ribs of the corrugated pipe.

There was no moon. Only starlight reflected off the scarred faces of mountain peaks in the distance. I had a feeling that the road might dead-end any second, but then the tree cover broke open onto a dark valley.

It's the only place in that valley, right after the bend in the old road.

I took one last hit of the joint, plucked the roach into the ditch, and kept going in the direction of the peaks, where eventually the road dwindled to scratches in the granite.

I came upon the bend at the edge of a pasture and caught a glimpse of a rusted roof. At the bottom of an overgrown drive lay the house, its back turned to the world. No sign read *No Trespassing*, but everything about the place said *Keep Out*: cattle wire all around, ragweed higher than my head, no lights, not a sound.

I climbed over the gate, walking through waist-high cheat grass along a mud drive cut into two deep furrows by centuries of truck and wagon wheels, and the shoulder of the house came into view with its hulking, twisted walls of crumbling adobe. I was high and I was horny, and the house was just as she had described it. I followed the drive around the side and Oppie sniffed away into a thick hedgerow.

The front of the house was L-shaped, one long, straight section of sagging mud rooms with an addition of rough timber protruding from the end. The boarded-up windows made me think of a face bandaged after a beating.

An open portal on the inside of the L, with its bowed posts and peeled-back tin roofing, wasn't doing much to hold up the rooms. The decking was riddled with splintered, rotting boards. A porch swing hung from rusty chains, hopelessly desolate on the threshold of this ruin.

As a precaution I grunted, "Hello." Silence. I stepped onto the portal and looked through the slats on the boarded windows.

The heart of the house was dark. I hadn't brought a flashlight, but I did have the camera. I held it at arm's length through the slats and fired the flash on the abandoned room, burning a brief image of squalor into my retina: floor covered with empty bottles and trash, planks full of jagged holes, and, in the corner, a discarded mattress blackened with filth, moldy stuffing erupting from a gash in its side.

Nothing was happening. Nobody home.

I am one hundred miles from Los Alamos—two hundred miles by road—and eight thousand feet low-down in the mountains in the middle of nowhere. Is it because I thought that a bunch of horny girls were going to be around here getting drunk without any guys their own age? Because I thought that I was going to bust out a joint and they were going to get uninhibited? Because I thought I was going to take pictures of it all? I did think that. Something about the way she said, *We should hook up.*

On the other side of this barren peak, back up on the Hill, I would be watching Letterman about now, actually half-watching and half-wishing I had porn channels, while Kitty lies curled up with flatulent Oppie on the far side of the king-size, springless, formaldehyde-free mattress.

A pudgy blood tech in black scrubs shakes her ass

at me, and I drag wife and dog on a miserable camping trip without provisions on a slim-to-none hunch. I set up a tent beside a remote hellhole on Fourth of July so I can sneak out to a house, an abandoned house, on a thin whiff of the possibility of *hooking up* where I wouldn't even have given a second look twenty years ago.

I held the camera out to take a picture of myself. The flash hit me full in the face. *This is to remind you what a loser looks like.*

I decided I might as well take a closer look.

I should have felt fear, I know, in the face of the still, dark house. The front door had been removed altogether and the entryway was a gaping hole.

It was pitch-black inside with all the windows boarded up. But when I stepped across the threshold I felt an instant, soporific comfort. There was a sudden drop of pressure in my chest accompanied by a great fatigue. I couldn't say what about the place made me feel as though my system was suddenly going to sleep, made me wish there was a chair to sit in.

I fired the flash into the other rooms. The first was actually an attached log cabin that hadn't been chinked in decades, gaps between the logs big enough to stick your hand through. Of the six adobe rooms, five connected end-to-end with no doors on the passages between them. But at the entrance to the last room, a heavy wooden door was deadbolted.

I wondered about the people who had lived here. These houses, these old adobes, were originally one-room dwellings. People ate and washed, slept, fucked, shat in the pot, gave birth, and died all between the same four walls.

It was only when the oldest son grew up that they converted a window on one end into a door or broke through a wall shotgun-style and added three more. The young man and his new wife moved into the next room, which they in turn filled with children, and the cycle began again.

In warmer months, the cooking and washing took place outside and naturally so did most of the work: farming, herding, and gathering the next winter's wood, a chore that began early in spring, as soon as the snow had melted from the last winter.

At eight thousand feet, winters lasted half the year—long, monotonous battles of resistance against the snow, the cold, the wind, the dark. The women melted snow in iron pots and cooked dried meat, chiles, beans, hominy. For six frigid months the families slept long hours, played tired games, told stories, and never let the fire go out.

I walked back out on the portal, heard Oppie rustling in the dark trees, and whistled low. "C'mere, boy."

He came out of the hedge dragging a plastic bag around his neck.

"Oppie, what the fuck did you get into?"

It was a large shopping bag, not quickie-mart sized but the kind you'd get at a department store.

"Drop!" He did not drop. "Drop, Oppie!" He could not drop. He had somehow gotten his pointy head through both handles, and now the bag was slung around his neck.

I bent over Oppie and he had a bizarre look in his eyes. I took the bag off his neck and felt that it was heavy. Oppie scrambled away.

I opened the bag and held the camera inside. The lighted display shone on an intricate pattern. I felt the lining of my throat thicken. Inside the bag were bones— not from a chicken or pig, but large bones, a tangle of eight or more.

I threw the bag back into the weeds and peered around the overgrown yard. The sagebrush and ragweed glowed dimly in the starlight. A cricket chirped loudly near my feet.

"Come on, Oppie, let's get back to the campground."

We walked back the way we had come.

When we got to the campground Kitty was still asleep. Oppie followed me into the tent and curled up at her feet. I slid quietly into my sleeping bag and lay awake a long time.

I played the scene over and over in my head: Oppie dragging a bag of bones out of the thicket. Had there been someone out there? Oppie hadn't growled. Could he have sniffed around in the brush, found the bag, and looped his head through the handles while trying to get at the contents? What kind of bones were they? Cow? Elk?

Toward dawn, with the crickets giving way to the birds, the insomnia yielded to a throbbing headache. I think of that dark hour waiting for sunrise—tossing in the sleeping bag, irritated by Oppie's farts, and wincing against the migraine—as a kind of haven, a last quiet before I came to understand the nightmare I had stumbled into.

S oon it was morning and kids were waking up at campsites all around us, laughing, screaming, jumping in the lake. It was a workday, but we were in no hurry. I had used a personal day to make my birthday a four-day weekend. Great expectations.

"This place is a dump," I told Kitty after taking Oppie for his walk. "Let's go home."

"You drag me way the fuck out here in the sticks and now you want to leave already?"

"There's no coffee and I have a headache."

"You and your goddamn headaches."

We packed out what we packed in and rattled back out of Morphy Lake State Park over that abysmal road, Kitty and I stewing in silence while Oppie stewed noisily.

When we got down from Ledoux, I made a left onto 518, pulled into the Mustang in Mora, and got some awful coffee. We crossed the mountains through Carson National Forest, blowing by Tres Ritos and Sipapu. I made a left onto 75 in Vadito, taking the winding state highway through Peñasco and Dixon.

Today is 7/5, you're going seventy-five on 75, and you just turned forty years old.

I made a left onto 68 in Embudo and we snaked through the canyon. We climbed out at Velarde and motored across the hot valley of Alcalde, then got onto 30 in Española and made our way through Santa Clara and San Ildefonso. We climbed 502 back up the Hill, all the way home Kitty's silent treatment accusing me: *Why didn't we stay in a hotel? We don't have to be camping. We have money.*

I am a reporter, among the best in the in-house publishing industry. I could be doing interviews for *Vogue* or *Vanity Fair*, but after the last wave of layoffs I decided to weather the recession on the richest hill in America, Los Alamos, writing profiles for *Surge*, the Lab's employee magazine. How many places in the world can a writer take frequent afternoons off and they still pay him enough to keep a restored Spider on the road?

I had the contract, the health plan, cost-of-living increases, grade-level adjustments, pay raises, bonuses, and the 401(k), on top of which I had already saved six figures.

When we got home, Kitty took Oppie for a walk on Pajarito Road.

I had agreed to a dog on the condition that it be a Basenji. I read somewhere that purebred Basenjis don't bark. Oppie didn't have to. Even though his low growl was barely audible over the hum of the refrigerator, he skittered around crazily on the linoleum whenever anyone came to the door, and that was enough watchdog for Los Alamos, where a lot of people don't even bother to lock their doors.

From the day we brought Oppie home, he had been surprisingly well mannered—except for the containment issue. But with the invisible fence he was adapting.

I took my statins and checked the cut on my hand. It was sore, but on the surface it didn't look so bad. I discarded the duct-taped tissue and dressed the wound with a sterile gauze pad.

I caught the weekend highlights on Golf Network while Kitty chopped Oppie some sirloin and popped a frozen pizza in the oven for us. I sat on the couch and she took the easy chair. More silent treatment while we watched a rerun of *Sex in the City*.

Remember when we used to watch TV together and cuddle on the couch and she would stroke my forearm, how I actually used to feel that? Now I don't feel anything at all. It's like it all happens in a movie, detached, without sensation. Why is that?

We polished off a bottle of good Shiraz with a couple of thin slices of pizza apiece. I scraped the cheese off mine. I had to watch the HDLs and the LDLs. We want to see the one go up and the other go down, said Dr. Hank, just like the scales of justice. I gave the crusts to Oppie. Back when Kitty and I used to speak to each other, we would call these pizza bones.

At bedtime Kitty went upstairs, popped an Ambien, and climbed under the covers, Oppie curling up at her feet.

I programmed Mr. Coffee and went upstairs to lie beside Kitty for a minute. Sometimes, on the edge of sleep, the Ambien would make her pliant, but tonight she was all elbows.

When I got the job in Los Alamos, the real-estate agent had left Kitty and me alone in this bedroom to share our images of the future together. Kitty tickled my ribs. Can we really afford it? Of course not, but that never stops anyone. This was 2007, and as long as you kept your credit somewhat clean, a broker could get you a loan based on stated income.

In better days we had lain side-by-side in the showroom on the king-size, springless, formaldehyde-free mattress, giggling and selecting our own Sleep Numbers. We bought king-size for luxury, but now when I tried getting close to her, all that size felt like we were in two beds, separated by a red zone in the middle that neither of us crossed with even a stray hand or foot.

I didn't like feeling sorry for myself, but I couldn't really blame Kitty. It wasn't that I hated her, even though I couldn't vouchsafe the opposite. *He never gave you a child*— her mother's indictment. Kitty never told her about the complicated miscarriage and how that pretty much cut off any possibility. Now Oppie offered all the worries and joys of parenthood—nursing, potty training, private schooling, grooming—compressed into a 15 percent lifespan.

Dropping off to sleep, I was thinking about the abandoned house. It had been strange about the bones around Oppie's neck, but this was nothing compared to the shock I would get when I checked out the photo I had taken of myself on the portal, the loser shot.

I awoke in the night to full alertness, stirred by a distant, persistent dog barking. My injured hand was throbbing. Kitty lay slack in Ambien's embrace and I needed to take a piss. The crickets were still going strong, so I knew it was sometime in the middle of the night. I felt for the bedside clock and squinted at the red numbers in the dark.

2:47—shit.

3:47 I could have handled, 4:47 might have been fine, and 5:47 would have been perfect, but after that sleepless night on the hard ground beside Morphy Lake, 2:47 meant a miserable day ahead.

I went downstairs without a shirt on. Oppie followed and I let him out the dining room slider. The house was quiet.

I lumbered into the bathroom and sat on the toilet. The statins gave me nocturnal erections, so I had to sit to piss if I didn't want to spray all over the place. I flipped on the light, *plink*. The little voice inside my head said, *Poor Dad*.

My father would wake up for work in the middle of the night and walk down the hallway to the bathroom. There was that second before he shut the door when he would flip the switch, flooding the hallway with light and making me squeeze my eyes shut. The worst part was that sound, echoing off tile every day except Sunday while he started his workday in the dark—*plink!*

I used to feel sorry for him for his sadness, for being already unhappy as long as I could remember, for his constant struggle to make ends meet. And I resented him for not being around more, for never taking me to a ball game, for always being drunk on Sunday and most nights after work.

Now that I was married I pitied my father for having stuck around. Why had he worked so hard when my mom had never shown any love for him? She hadn't even been nice to him.

What made him wake up at an hour when most dads, even those with happy families, were asleep, and what made him get out of bed, walk past mean, crazy, sleeping Mom, come over to my bed, and, while I pretended to sleep, lay a hand on my head . . . then go into the bathroom, throw the switch, and give himself a shave in the middle of the night?

What made him get going on the first in a haul of chores through a workday that he couldn't have enjoyed, that nobody could, through long, monotonous days of commute, back-breaking work, and slow, halting, drunken returns?

And then came Fair Oaks, the institution. The one time I had asked him about it, he said it was because he had begun having terrible nightmares and that after a while, even on the brightest days, he couldn't stop thinking about them.

Dad's psychiatrist had been an Italian American, the brother of a famous character actor in the movies. Now every time I see that actor in a modern mafia movie, I think of the doctor, placid behind wire-rimmed glasses, prescribing mountains of lithium, four hospitalizations, thirteen bipolar shock treatments. This was before re-searchers discovered that unipolar ECT was just as ef-fective and fried memory a lot less permanently. But don't resent the doctor for his orders. He was just trying to jolt Dad out of those nightmares.

Finally, my father's funeral—devastating, but also a relief. When I had gone past the casket and made the sign of the cross, I heard that noise of the bathroom light switch: *plink*. Now every time I hear it, it's like the sound of a little coffin shutting. *Poor Dad.*

I went into the living room and turned on the TV, muted it. The Golf Network was cycling the same highlights show as when I had gone to bed. My hand throbbed. The couch was hard. The upholstery was cold.

I turned off the TV, went into the dining room, and flipped on the back flood lamps. I pushed aside the cur-tain and caught Oppie squatting on my practice putting green. I rolled up a copy of *Surge* and threw open the slider, smacking Oppie's haunches as the final squirt dribbled onto the grass.

That's when I remembered the photo.

I went to the garage and got the camera from the glove compartment of the Spider. I connected it, woke up the laptop, and opened iPhoto. I had not emptied the memory card in a while. *You have 112 new photos. Download now?* Yes.

I went to the cabinet to pour myself a glass of scotch. Then I opened the desk drawer and took out my stash and papers and rolled myself a joint. While the pho-tos downloaded I smoked. First there were a bunch of pictures of the workers digging the trench on our prop-erty line for the invisible fence, then a bunch more shots that Kitty took of Oppie playing on the front lawn. Then the download got to the picture I took at the house, the loser shot.

In the photo—*holy shit!*—a spike of red light seemed to shoot out of my chest.

Oo-ee-oo.

I peered at the photo and tried to make sense of how it happened: had it been digital noise, or maybe the flash reflecting off the zipper of my jacket? It's not unusual for photos taken in low light to develop artifacts, but this was a straight red spike, and it was right there over my heart, a real *you gotta put dat up on your Facebook* shot.

I needed to show this to someone for a reality check, but if I showed it to Kitty I would have to explain my late-night hike at the campground. I decided I would wait and show Hank Farmer for a second opinion.

I closed the laptop and went upstairs to lie next to Kitty. When I heard a scratch on the dining room slider, I remembered Oppie and went back downstairs to let him in.

I lay back down beside Kitty with my statin erection and thought about the blood tech. When would I go back into the clinic for the next draw? I could probably squeeze one in before the end of the month. What would the blood tech tell me? *Sorry, my car broke down . . . ?* Would she even remember? Was this something she did to guys regularly, or was she fucking with me specifically?

Except for the goth stuff, she seemed like a typical employee of the valley, another one of those Hispanas who take all the menial jobs at the Lab. They were the new migrant workers, people who race up the mesa every day from forty or sixty miles away because there aren't any houses for less than a mil on the Hill.

She was one of those women that northern New Mexico is built upon, paraprofessionals, whatever that means, working long days while their boyfriends stay home drunk or go out for irregular day labor and complain about how they can never get a break. It was possible she had pegged me as a potential sugar daddy but then one of those guys whose name was tattooed on her arm discovered the scheme from one of her girlfriends and beat it right out of her.

The throbbing hand kept me up most of the night. Only when the first light of dawn began glowing against the curtains did I finally begin feeling drowsy. I lay there a long time and thought about the house.

Maybe this was one point where it might have been possible to let it go. The house had given me a strange feeling, but it could have remained a quirky accident. The photo could have stayed there on the memory card, unlooked at for months, years, and the bones around Oppie's neck remained something unexplained, barely remembered, just another paranormal holiday in New Mexico. But I was hooked. Something was already growing inside of me.

I was jolted awake by the keening of a Weedwacker. I got up to look out the window. My neighbor Ned was edging his lawn in gloves, goggles, ear protection. I looked at the clock—6:20 a.m. This is insane. What kind of asshole weed-whacks at 6:20 in the morning?

I remembered getting up in the night, remembered the photo, and decided to catch a round down at Buffalo Thunder before rolling up on Dr. Hank at brunch for Bloody Marys.

I showered and got dressed. Then I went down to the kitchen and poured a cup from Mr. Coffee, took one scorching sip, and left the mug in the sink. I packed the laptop in my briefcase, loaded my clubs in the trunk of the Spider, and backed out of the garage into the Los Alamos sun.

I was at the light on the corner of Third and Main listening to the idle of the Spider. The opposing pedestrian countdown told me there were only seconds left on my red when an old man stepped off the curb wearing something he'd tailored from a burlap bag, the collar and sleeves scissored out of the bottom and sides, the hem of the sack riding above his bony knees like a tattered miniskirt.

I said to myself, *Great, the sackcloth-and-ashes people are back.*

He was a perfect specimen: stringy hair, wild eyes,

crazy beard. The old man intercepted a woman jogging on the crosswalk. "There's blood on your shoes!" he yelled at her, shaking a bag that discharged a little cloud of ashes over her New Balances.

The jogger dodged and the old man swung his fishy eye on me. "There's blood on your car!" He pitched toward the Spider and I had to look away. The skinny legs reminded me unpleasantly of my dad in a towel coming out of the shower.

The light turned green and I leaned on the horn. For such a small car, it had a solid old Italian air horn, and the old man jumped out of the way.

Here was one of the little disturbing nuisances of life on the Hill that you had to learn to push into the periphery this time of year. What was Pax Kyrie doing back so soon? There were still ten days until the anniversary of the first nuclear detonation at the Trinity site. Sackcloth-and-ashes season usually began around July 16, the birthday of the Bomb, and wound down three weeks later on Hiroshima Day, but it seemed like every year the freaks from Pax Kyrie were coming to town a little earlier.

First a couple of stragglers started hanging out at Ashley Pond with their signs and their leaflets, then small bunches of them appeared around town spouting their holy ramblings, and finally a few hundred of them converged for a "die-in" that tied up traffic. It was pretty funny seeing them lying down on the roadsides in their sackcloths. They looked like a bunch of cavemen who had gotten tired waiting for the bus.

The sackcloth-and-ashers weren't so different from right-to-lifers. In Pax Kyrie's skewed perspective, everyone on the Hill was an abortionist. I wanted to propose an epigram for a monument that would greet them at the bottom of the Hill before they made the climb: *Yes, this is the town that built the Bomb. Get over it.*

I drove down to the valley. I had the radar detector on, but it didn't pick up the waves quickly enough for me to decelerate to less than seventy before passing a sheriff's car tucked behind a knoll at the safety corridor. Lucky for me the deputy seemed to be snoozing.

I slowed down in plenty of time for the tribal police officer at the edge of San Idelfonso and kept it at fifty-five for the last ten miles to Pojoaque. *Win a Chevy Truck* at Cities of Gold Sports Bar. *Dos Manos Repo 19.99* at Koko-man, and remember, *Don't take chex from Teresa O Estrada.*

At the self-serve car wash, the low-riders eyed me uncertainly. My black Spider was a fly ride, but the cholos couldn't be sure whether it was macho like a Charger or gay like a Porsche. I hosed off the dust from the miserable camping trip and found a Mexican who gave it a soft shammying for an extra buck, shining the black finish up like an eight ball.

I drove out to the Towa Golf Resort and got my irons from the back. My hand was still tender from the tent-stake injury, but with gloves on my stroke was in good form.

On the third fairway there was nobody behind me and I was out of sight of the clubhouse when I reached into the ball pocket of the golf bag and pulled out an Altoids tin. The joints in there looked just like wooden tees: white and thin as nails, slightly tapered at the end. I lit one and smoked.

I thought about the blood tech and considered the

possibility of stopping at nine holes and driving to Rinconada to see her. Was the clinic even open on Saturday? I
didn't think I could pull off dropping by without seem-
ing pathetic. Either she had spaced out on her invitation
or I had gotten caught up in some bitchy, goth-Hispanic
dissimulation: *Fuck you, gringo, if you're stupid enough to think
I'm going to meet your skinny ass in the middle of the night in the
middle of the woods on the Fourth of July!*

My injured hand started throbbing again, and two
pueblo bison humping on the thirteenth fairway threw
me into a funk.

I cut the round short, packed my irons in the Spider, and drove the winding road back up 502, passing
beneath the billboard for Los Alamos Medical Center.
Jack and Jill Went Up the Hill to Take Mommy to Her Mammogram.

Down in Henry Farmer's basement, but don't call it that. The rec room, the tavern, the lodge, the nineteenth hole—whatever the designation of the week to obscure his disappointment that it was only a finished basement.

Mixing Stoli with V8 in a pitcher, Dr. Hank said, "Ever wonder why there aren't any real bars on the Hill?"

"Yeah, why is that?"

"We have bars in our homes instead. Los Alamos County has the nation's most million-dollar rec rooms per capita." Farmer, who on weekdays doubles as my physician, flipped the power strip on the bar back and three store-bought neon signs illuminated the Sheetrock. "Well, old boy, here's to trying to quit."

He poured me a Bloody Mary, but something about seeing those bison humping had left me feeling sullen. "No thanks."

"What do you mean?"

"I quit."

"You can't quit!"

"Why not? That's the toast, isn't it?"

"The toast is here's to *trying* to quit! Don't be a quitter. The point is to keep trying." He poured another for himself. "Anyway, what about this photo?"

"First, let me tell you about the miserable camping trip. It starts with my blood tech."

"Your what?"

"At the clinic where I get my draws."

"A blood tech? You kinky fucking pervert!"

"It's the statins you prescribe me."

"The statins? You'd take any piece of ass whether or not you were on heart medication."

"You're the one who told me about the side effects, Hank. You're my doctor."

"Speaking of which, let me see that hand." He peeked under the bandage. The tent-stake wound was still pretty sore. "Have you had a tetanus shot in the past seven years?"

"You tell me. I'm coming in for test results next week."

"Keep that thing clean in the meantime."

Farmer's wife called downstairs from the kitchen: "Should I set an extra place for brunch?"

"Leave us alone! We're classified in here!" Hank hates it when Mary reminds him that his bar is just a fancy cellar.

"The blood tech held my arm and told me, *You want to hook up at this lake?* Hook up: that means sex, right?"

"Does she have a big butt?"

"She's what you'd call a goth. Tattoos, pierced tongue, keeps her fingernails long and painted black."

"A goth blood tech?" Farmer slurped his drink. "Only in New Mexico!"

"She told me about this place near Morphy Lake where she said her girlfriends go to party. *We bring a bottle*, she said. *You should come.*"

"You should come!"

"That's what she said!"

I woke up my laptop and rubbed my hands together.

It was going to be a good show. I sipped my drink, and since then I can't help connecting the taste of the Bloody Mary to the beginning of the trouble.

When I double-clicked the iPhoto icon, the system skipped a beat.

"Come on," I coaxed. I slugged my drink to keep myself from keying force quit.

"What are we supposed to be looking at, anyway? Dirty pictures?" Farmer asked. "Don't show me any pornography unless they say they're eighteen."

"No. There's just this one strange shot of me."

"I don't think I want to see any strange shots of you."

"Not that kind of strange."

While Farmer poured us each another drink, I finally did try to force quit, but nothing could stop the spinning beach ball of death.

None of the key combos to warm-boot OS X could break the ice, so I finally held the power button for a hot shutdown.

I waited ten seconds, restarted, and that was that. When the screen lit back up, the monitor was blue and all I got was the question mark of total annihilation.

Farmer said, "You probably got a virus from downloading so much foreign porn."

"Is it noon yet?"

"Quarter to."

"Gotta go. I'm going to take this down to Comp-Medic."

"Here, at least take your drink with you."

I raced the Spider downtown, a Bloody Mary in one of Farmer's to-go cups sloshing in the little hole on the armrest.

At CompMedic I watched from inside a fluorescent daze while the geek booted it up with a utility disk and confirmed my worst fears: "Absolute, unrecoverable disk failure."

"Can't you back up the data?"

"Sorry, no data left to back up. This crash left no survivors."

The laptop was no longer under warranty, and I had declined the manufacturer's three-year protection plan. The geek charged me fifty bucks.

"You're lucky. It's Saturday, so if you'd come in after noon it would have triggered an emergency-room fee."

After tossing back the rest of the Bloody Mary, I drove to Smith's for a Mike's Hard Lemonade and drank it in the parking lot.

The Lab issued me the cleared PC for home-office use, but I had bought myself the laptop, and it was supposed to have been all mine.

It was going to be my mistress, that laptop, the kind of affair where you stay up all night together. I had fantasized about the screenplay I would write in my off time. I imagined walking to the far reaches of the parking lot on my lunch breaks just to spend twenty minutes in the car with her. But that's all there had been to it: my imagination.

I had gotten nothing better on that hard drive over the past few years than one document titled *Document* with a few times, dates, and dits:

11:30 p.m., June 4: The beginning.
4:00 a.m., August 12: Can't sleep.
6:15 p.m., November 30: Telephone, brb.

It was all worthless, just a bag of bones.

There were a few hundred photos on the laptop that I hadn't backed up, but most of them were of Kitty and Oppie. The biggest loss had been the loser shot. Now I couldn't remember whether I had deleted the original from the camera.

I thought about when Kitty and I had started taking those photos. When we first came to town, I dropped her off at CB Fox to shop and took myself on a drive, crawling up Central Avenue at twenty-five miles per hour. I remember an old guy on a bike shouting, "Slow down!" Wow, I said to myself, I've really arrived.

I went to the end of Central and turned around at Ashley Pond. I could have gone back down Trinity, but on a hunch I turned onto Deacon instead, that Steely Dan song in my head. Nothing happening here, just the back of a Mexican restaurant, specials advertised on a Coke sign, and a bunch of parking lots. Where were the posters for Corona, Tecate, and Negra Modelo? Where was the neon *Cocktails* sign?

That's when I saw Central Avenue Grille, but when I parked at Starbucks and walked back to peek in, the only people in there at happy hour were the waiter and a young couple with two kids sitting at a table, the dad drinking Diet Coke, the whole scene depressing me.

In desperation, I drove back down the road to Smith's and read against the stucco storefront: *Deli, Bakery, Pharmacy, Food Court, 1-Hour Photo*—but there was no sign that said *Beer & Wine*, much less *Spirits*. What the fuck was wrong with this place?

Hope dwindling, I pulled into the parking lot, and thank god there was a liquor department. I almost hugged a stocker. I bought a twenty-four-ounce Bud Lime just to calm myself down.

It had almost been easier to find weed. I had a nasty habit of paying more for naturopathy, and marijuana was my mood-booster. True, I had the Lab health plan, so pharmaceuticals were just five bucks a bottle. I could ask Dr. Hank for a scrip, stop in at Walgreens for some antidepressants, and walk out with fifty little pills that were ten times more psychoactive than ganja, chasing them in plain daylight with a tall latte from Starbucks while my neighbors smiled and asked me about my golf game. But I chose to sneak around and pay extra for pot on the belief that if it grows in the earth, it can't be all that bad for you.

There was no way I could buy from anyone who lived anywhere near the Hill. Maybe you could if you were a division leader or an insider at the Lab, but not me. I couldn't risk my clearance status. The DOE doesn't take casual drug use lightly. They actually send a recreational vehicle equipped with a mobile blood-draw unit around to the different divisions at random intervals to screen employees. But I was fortunate to have one of the few jobs at the Lab where you didn't get surprise tests.

I was a journalist, not a scientist, and so I fell through a crack between clearance levels. I had done the screening upon hire, after a week of detox shakes, and I wouldn't have to go through it again unless I got involved in a workplace accident, which would be unlikely since on any given day I handled no instrument more dangerous than a pen. The drug-test RV never stopped at *Surge*.

After a quick search on WeBeKind.com, I had found the address for Mar Iguana Smoke Shop in Española. I knew I couldn't just pop in and ask for a connect, so I parked outside and waited until I saw my mark.

It was strange to be doing this all over again. Twenty years in my university town had made buying pot on the way home Friday night as easy as a beeper callback:

pick up beer, chips, then marijuana. I watched the door of Mar Iguana for a while. I didn't feel like dealing with any of the local vatos, but I knew a hippie would show up eventually.

Sure enough, along came a bearded old mountain man wearing a dingy tie-dye. I waited until he emerged with his rolling papers and approached him at his beat-up van.

"Excuse me, brother, but would you happen to know where I can get some medicine?" (I had picked up this lingo from WeBeKind.)

"You some kinda fuckin' narc?"

"No, sir, just new here in New Mexico, and I don't know how long it will take to get my green card."

"Well, don't waste your time on that shit unless you want the man to fuck with your supply. Follow me, and if you are a fuckin' narc I'll shoot you and bury you where nobody will ever find you."

Lucky timing, Mel Woburn told me later, because he doesn't make it down from Abiquiu but once a month for supplies and he grows the best shit in the Sangre de Cristo.

Now, in the Smith's parking lot at the bottom of my hard lemonade, I should have let it go. I should have settled into my job at the Lab and never looked back.

Maybe if I hadn't driven out to Abiquiu I would have forgotten all about my Fourth of July weekend. But when I checked the Altoids tin and saw how little weed was left, I decided to go see Mel. I had no idea how that filthy trailer in the badlands would lead me back to the abandoned house in Ledoux, would drop me right in the middle of the nightmare.

I drove out Highway 84 and stopped at Bode's for beer. When I pulled into the parking lot, the sun reflecting off my fender flashed on two young boys crouched in front of the store in tattered shorts. I walked past and the boys looked up from a pothole filled with muddy rainwater. They were torturing something, drowning something, something small that splashed frantically in the puddle. They turned back to their work, intent as surgeons.

A few minutes later I came out with my sack and again the boys looked up, staring at me like they were sizing me up for one of their experiments. I started the car and turned a tight circle to get back out on Highway 84, kicking up enough dust that I knew I would already have to get the Spider waxed again.

A couple of miles off the highway, down a dirt road, up on rusty jacks between an irrigation ditch and an arroyo—it was here sometime in the mid-'70s that Mel Woburn ended up scuttling his trailer. Behind it rose an ancient rock fifty million years old that had once showed up in the background of a famous photo by Georgia O'Keeffe, but Mel's trailer was well concealed from the road by a tangle of scrub oaks that grew in the arroyo, and now somewhere back there in the desert Mel teased enough water from a spring to grow his killer marijuana.

I pulled in behind the trees. When I shut off the engine the crickets took over. The sun was beginning its descent in the west, and it was cooler up here, like it had been at the campground in Mora but without the humidity of the lake.

I walked up to the trailer with the six-pack. A rusted metal drum overflowing with crushed Milwaukee's Best cans stood outside the door, and inside I could hear the Mexican station blasting. I banged on the storm door, but I couldn't hit it hard enough for Mel to hear me through the wall of mariachi horns and drums. I had to wait for the break between songs.

The song ended with a fusillade of sound effects— lasers, sirens, and a long, ominous explosion. I opened the storm door and waited for the split-second lapse after the throaty station ID—*Este es el Big Bro-der de la radio raza, noventa-y-dos-punto-nueve ¡Radio Oso!*—to rap sharply on the window of the steel door.

The next mariachi was cut short at the *rat-tat-tat* of a snare intro when Mel killed the radio and a second later pushed aside the curtain with the barrel of his .22. Bleary and skittish, he looked cockeyed at me. I opened the sack and held up the beer: Bohemia. The corner of Mel's mouth twitched in recognition, the curtain dropped, and I heard the door unlatch.

The dark, hot room stank of smoke, sweat, and rotten fruit that had been lost in the chaos of clothing piles, stacks of old papers, scattered cassette tapes, and plastic tape cases clouded with dust. On the fireplace mantle stood a wooden crucifix draped by crisscrossed bandoleers packed with shotgun shells.

Mel staggered across the room and sank back into the cushions of his tattered sofa, where he slept beneath wrinkled *Hustler* centerfolds pinned to the wall.

He leaned the .22 against the arm of the sofa and turned the radio back up to a moderate blare.

I sat on the straight-back chair, took a lighter from his table, and levered open a beer. Mel accepted it without comment, upending it like a marathon runner at the end of the race, his Adam's apple bobbing up and down on his fat, grizzled neck while the first twelve ounces hit home.

He croaked, "Cold—good."

I pried open another, handed it over, and opened one for myself.

Mel slid down to the other end of the sofa to throw another log in the stove. No fridge, phone, or electricity out here—just the battery-powered radio, which he kept on the Mexican station. It's not because he spoke Spanish—he didn't—or particularly enjoyed the music; it was white noise for him, twenty-four hours of it in this room of dark-paneled walls and blackout curtains, and it was guaranteed that whenever there was a deejay interlude, newsbreak, or other announcement, he wouldn't understand enough to get an impression of something, anything, going on in the outside world.

"Had this whore here last night." By whore he meant woman. "Kicked that bitch out about an hour ago. Ugly as hell, but she sucked cock all right. Thought you might have been her come back for more."

Mel guzzled his second beer. Once in a while I asked myself, *Why do I come all the way out to Abiquiu to visit Mel Woburn?* I hated some things about the way Mel came on—the misogyny, the cranky paranoia—making each pilgrimage for more homegrown like a ritual rehashing of what had gone wrong with the '60s. Each time I came here I had been patronizing Mel, leading him to believe I was interested in his crazy hippie days, when privately I pitied him for being such a burnout recluse, but there was nobody in Los Alamos I could speak freely with about my fondness for marijuana.

I opened us each another beer—he kept it so hot in the trailer it was easy to put away a few fast—and asked, "How was your Fourth?"

Mel made a *voilà* gesture across the trailer, his fingertips charred to nubs from stoking all the fires he stoked, smoking all the pot he smoked. "Same old, same old." He started to roll a joint.

Going to Mel was a little like church for me. There was ritual, there were parables, and of course we shared the sacrament. And there was something else Mel and I shared, a disease that infected men like us, making us waste ourselves, our talents, our days, on tired schemes and cheap tricks, burning ourselves up inside, meanwhile tarring up our lungs and pickling our livers, putting the brain slowly to sleep. Maybe I did it with a little more style: imported whiskey and bottled beer with the gold foil on the neck instead of Milwaukee's Best; the expensive house and the moping trophy-wife instead of hippie whores and a bent-up trailer with centerfolds above the sofa. Otherwise, the only thing that made us different was that, in the midst of all the dissipation, I kept paying taxes.

"How 'bout you," Mel said, "what'd you do?"

"Went camping in Ledoux."

Mel licked the fresh spliff. "Morphy Lake?"

"Yeah. You been there?"

"First place I came back in '69."

"No shit?"

"Would I shit you? All kinds of hippies lived out there. Used to crash at a big adobe above the lake."

"An L-shaped place?"

"Yep. Part of it was actually a log cabin." Mel shook his head and lit the joint. He puffed and passed.

"What brought you out there?" I hit the joint.

"There was no more room at the Hog Farm. One night smoking around a campfire in Llano, a hippie told me, *Go to Mora. There's a big house that always has room up there.* I found this one whore I liked a little more than the rest, and that place in Ledoux is where we ended up shacking up, the Johnson ranch."

"Johnson?"

"Johnson—old man who built the place, long time before the hippies got hold of it."

When I passed the joint back our fingers touched, and I somehow understood that this relationship was now no longer just about replenishing my pot supply. It was about a particular abandoned house one hundred miles, as the crow flies, from here, almost two hundred over the roads.

In the clarity of the moment, I found that I no longer felt patronizing toward Mel. On the contrary, I envied something of him: his story.

Mel seemed to take note of this shift in my estimation, and for the first time I noticed a sly smile forming in the corners of his crusty eyes.

"It was nice out there at the Johnson ranch: big house, lots of rooms, people cutting wood, trying to make something happen. We had chickens, horses, gardening in the summer. It was just after Woodstuck—'scuze me:

stock—and we were still going strong, even when Wavy and all the Hog Farmers flew back to Frisco. We were the true believers. Little Joe, Crazy Jane, Sunshine, and Ritchie Motherfucker all made that scene . . ."

I threw two twenties on the table. "Are any of them still around?"

"You mean alive, right? Ritchie's dead, Little Joe's in the lock-up for dealing, and Crazy Jane got institutionalized. Sunshine I haven't seen in thirty years. Last time was at a no-nukes rally in Albuquerque."

Mel stood and picked up the money nonchalantly. He shuffled to the kitchen, bellowing over the radio, "His real name is Shorn Anderson. It was Shawn, but he legally changed it on paper and everything on account of he once survived almost getting scalped by a mountain lion. Anyway, he always went by Sunshine."

Mel came back from the kitchen and tossed me a little baggie full of buds. "Never really wanted to go back to that place. A lot of weird shit happened there."

"What kind of weird shit?"

"When the hippies went to cremate Ritchie Motherfucker, they found out it isn't so easy to burn a body."

"Shit . . ."

We had worked down the joint, and now Mel pinched what was left in a pair of forceps, his roach clip.

"Ritchie fell off a horse and died of complications. It was Sunshine who came up with the idea for cremating him. I told him I wasn't having any part of it. I knew he was too fucked up to do it right. Ritchie was my friend. I thought we should have a rent party and get a collection together, at least get Ritchie a pine box. But Sunshine had a college textbook on religions of Southeast Asia that diagramed how the Sufis build a funeral pyre, and Little Joe and Crazy Jane went along with it."

I shuddered, hit the roach. "Fuck . . ."

"My bitch and me cleared the hell out of there and never went back, but I heard about it later from Little Joe. Sunshine built the pyre right—except for the height: it was supposed to be three meters, not three feet. There wasn't enough draft underneath to feed the fire. They just singed Ritchie's hair and sort of cooked him for a while. The stink must have been awful." Mel took one last puff, smudged the forceps in the ashtray, and added the roach to his pile on the bench. "Bad shit happened there. A lot worse shit than that. When you walk up to a house like that, walk away."

I got back in the car with my weed and a want for that story. The Sangre de Cristo Mountains loomed darkly in the east. On the other side of those peaks was the Johnson house. The story of Ritchie Mother-fucker made me want to take a closer look at the place, see if I could incorporate more detail into a magazine feature. I repeated the names to myself: *Sunshine, Little Joe, Ritchie Motherfucker.* Bad shit happened there.

On the outskirts of Española I thought about which turn to take. It wasn't so far from here to 68, then a short drive to 75, and then just twenty miles or so through Dixon and Peñasco to get to 76. From there the Spider could make it out to Mora in a little over an hour, then another hour up to Ledoux. I could stop at Walgreens and pick up some PowerBars to tide me over.

As I drove back through the badlands at twilight, the low sun illuminating the weather-baked chimineas outside Santa Clara and radiating heat at me through the bug-spattered windshield of the Spider, I decided if I wanted to get a better look at the house that I should visit during daytime. I got back on 502 and wound up the Hill to Los Alamos.

Kitty was asleep but Oppie greeted me excitedly before heading back to bed. I went into my study and put the dead laptop on the shelf. I rolled a joint and poured myself a scotch.

* * *

In bed Kitty was as good as dead to me. I lay there and let my mind's eye rise above Los Alamos and the mesa. I soared across the Española valley like a bird, flying over the Sangre de Cristo to look down on the other side of the mountain range. I saw the country around Ledoux. There was a round, cold lake. There was a high valley. There was a house.

I looked over at the numbers: 4:17. My hand was still sore and I knew I wouldn't get to sleep.

I remembered the photo that had fried my laptop. Was it still on the camera? I got out of bed and went down to my study.

When I tried to turn on the camera a bad feeling shot through me. It made a little noise, *peew*, and then the display went blank. It did not say, *CARD EMPTY*. It did not say anything. I tried a new set of batteries. Still nothing. Shit. Now both the camera and the laptop were fried.

I tried to get my mind off my string of bad luck by doing some research. Maybe I could learn more about Ritchie Motherfucker or Sunshine.

I woke up the PC and tried a Hail Mary by Googling *Ledoux* plus *Ritchie Motherfucker*. Zero hits.

I checked on Facebook, but there was no Shorn Anderson.

On a hunch I got on Yahoo! People Search and typed *Shorn Anderson* and *New Mexico*. Interesting: one record, no street address, in Pojoaque.

I got back on Google, typed *Sunshine* and *Pojoaque*, and found some crappy copy: *There's plenty o' sunshine to be found in the northern New Mexico town of Pojoaque . . .*

I tried *hippie Sunshine Pojoaque* and got a recent newsletter from the Santa Fe Chamber of Commerce with the headline: *Local Chef's Cooking Is Hallucinatory Hot!*

Pojoaque, NM. At the Roadrunner Diner on the main highway here, the short-order cook, who goes by the name "Sunshine," says he came way back with the hippies but stayed when he tried the chile.

Looked like a hit.

I went into the dining room and flipped on the back flood lamps, and then I remembered that Oppie had stayed up in bed with Kitty. I checked the latch on the slider and pulled the curtain all the way to the edge of the glass. Then I rolled a couple of joints and put the Altoids tin in my shirt pocket.

I went into the garage, backed the Spider out of the driveway, and wound downhill to the valley below, combing my hair in the rearview mirror.

The Roadrunner was open twenty-four hours and served breakfast every one of them. I would normally inquire of the waitress, just to be sure, whether there was an egg whites–only option for one of the scrambles, but I didn't want her asking (and annoying) the cook before I got a chance to meet him, and anyway a restaurant with a hand-decorated sign advertising a half-pound hamburger with pastrami did not seem like the kind of place that offered heart-healthy substitution.

I couldn't order nothing, either. That would be really annoying. I considered the grapefruit even though I hate grapefruit. I should get steak and eggs, right? The most deadly thing on the menu, just to broadcast to the cook that I am a regular guy: strong, tough, hungry.

I settled on black coffee and a bowl of oatmeal—bland, hearty, nonthreatening, like a Quaker. I didn't count on getting it with a hunk of margarine on top swimming in its own melt, reminding me of the cube of pork fat on the label of baked beans. I fished out what hadn't liquefied with my spoon and, lacking a saucer on which to put the goop, plopped it into my water glass.

I knew immediately that this had been a mistake, as I was thirsty and the glass was full. If I asked for more water, I would expose my bizarre behavior to the waitress and it might be relayed to the cook. Better to just sit here thirsty and get whatever information I could until the glass got bussed back to the kitchen. Let the dishwasher figure it out.

I put away half the porridge and could eat no more, so I asked the waitress if I could please speak to the cook for a moment. I thought I would go into it like an interview for a profile. J-school and editorial work had trained me not to pry, but instead to subtly suggest my own importance and allow the subject to volunteer information.

"Harold," she called, "someone out here wants to see you."

Harold? At first I thought I had the wrong day, the wrong guy. But even before I caught my first glimpse of my man, I remembered that this was America: so long as he had a Social Security number, a person could call himself whatever he wanted and change his name as often as he liked. In the land of payday stores and checks-cashed huts, you didn't even need ID that matched.

Through the order window to the kitchen, all I could see were his narrowed, bloodshot eyes and his hook nose marbled with ruptured vessels. He was not happy to be summoned. I knew he had to be my Sunshine.

When he came out to the counter and I got a good look at his face, the forehead and mouth didn't do much to improve the overall impression: bushy eyebrows, big scowl. He looked down at the counter and recognized me right away as Bowl of Oatmeal.

"Something wrong with your breakfast?" said Harold-Shorn-Sunshine.

"Not at all. In fact, it's excellent. Best oatmeal I ever had."

I forced another spoonful in my mouth and chewed quickly without swallowing. His eyes went to my water glass and he saw the glob of margarine congealed amidst the ice.

"What's the problem, pal?"

"No problem at all, really. My name is James."

I put out my hand, wrapped in gauze from the injury. He didn't shake it. He didn't even look at it. Some stranger comes up and asks for you at the Roadrunner Diner in Pojoaque, it could only be bad news, right? No news is good news: that's what makes us happy. News out of the blue is never good unless it's about an inheritance.

I could have mentioned the name Mel Woburn, but that might be someone Sunshine no longer considered a friend. When you don't know someone in this world, there is always the chance that you might meet one day and become friends; but once you did know a person, the likelihood was that you weren't going to stay friends forever, and then you'd have a history, and then you'd rather not hear about them.

I figured I would lay it out straight. "I wanted to ask you about this place in Ledoux called the Johnson house."

"Jesus Christ . . ." He glanced around and lowered his voice. "How'd you find me?"

"Yahoo! People Search."

"What the fuck you call me?"

"No, Yahoo! the web portal—it's just the name of a site on the Internet."

"I don't care what it is. How do I get off it?"

This was going poorly. I should have taken the alternate approach: come into the Roadrunner for several days in a row, allow him to approach me with some nicety—*Back five days in a row, you sure must like my cooking*—then make up something about a new job nearby, turn the conversation to weekends, and let drop that I recently went camping at a place called Morphy Lake. I would have kept the upper hand, and Sunshine would have told me whatever he knew about the Johnson house. But now I was on the wrong end of this interview, and for all I knew I was asking the wrong guy the wrong questions.

"Well, you don't really get off the Internet . . ." All of a sudden I saw an opportunity. Find the entrée by accident, figure out what the down-and-out informant wants, and get a foot in the door, make it into a fraternal exchange: this guy didn't know anything about the web. If I offer him an hour of computer consulting in exchange for the story of the house, maybe we would become pals after all. "Unless you create a decoy. I could take care of that for you."

"What'd you say your name was?"

"James."

"You know Red's in Española?"

"Sure, *Best Food in Town*."

He did not smile. "Meet me at the bar at lunchtime, alone."

Sunshine turned his back on me and returned to the kitchen, sliding the order window shut.

I stood up to leave and saw that the waitress had made herself scarce. All I had was a twenty and it was definitely time to go, although where to I didn't know. She ended up with a generous tip.

There would be six hours—the full morning—until the rendezvous at Red's. I could play a few rounds at

Towa Golf Resort, but my hand ached, the morning was already sweltering, and after the encounter with Sunshine my nerves were shot.

I killed a little time at a coffee shop called the Red Door and checked out my finances on the phone. It made me feel pretty good to look at the 100k I had socked away, all in a money market fund that back-ended my checking and savings accounts. I could have put some of it in stocks, but fuck that after 2008.

I stopped at Saints & Sinners but it wouldn't open until noon—goddamn Sunday blue laws. Fortunately, there was a guy behind the store who waved me over to his trailer. He sold me a couple of Jim Beam minis at a hefty mark-up.

I downed the Jim Beams in the parking lot of Lowe's and wandered around for a while inside the home-improvement warehouse. The bland prerecorded lady chanting *Assistance needed in the glass aisle* over and over was a perfect soundtrack for the seventh circle of hell.

I got back in the Spider, scanned the parking lot, took out the Altoids tin, and lit a joint.

I decided to drive up to Chimayó. Still three hours to kill. I thought it would be cool to visit the Santuario, no ordinary church but a "sanctuary" that, thanks to the magic dirt that comes out of a hole, draws millions of Christians a year—many who literally make the pilgrimage on hands and knees.

I parked a hundred yards up the highway from a church plaza choked with beat-up Continentals parked willy-nilly on the packed earth. I bowed my way into the chapel, tapping my shoulders and forehead in an effort to blend in. I wasn't looking for a revelation. The chapel just seemed like a nice, cool place to kill some time.

Behold the altar, the cross, the alcove off to the left wherein emerged the miraculous mud, walls featuring all the braces, crutches, walkers, and wheelchairs that the beneficiaries had left behind.

I read a retablo:

*Jesus saith unto him, Rise, take up thy bed, and walk.
And immediately the man was made whole, and took up his
bed, and walked.*

Beside it, incongruous among the orthopedic wares, hung a blue tennis racket. What had this devotee been cured of?

The priest was nowhere to be found, but a crazy old lady came up to me with her evil eye and said, "Maldito!" She made a cross over herself three times quickly as if to cleanse herself of me. "Get you-self a sanador, que te cante unos labados."

I got out of there quick, driving back to the state highway and down to Española.

Red's. Red's restaurant-lounge. Red's with the drive-up window attached: *Fairview Liquor Store & Bar, Dispenser Lic. #0331.*

Red's with the big neon sign flashing *Reds* and the cheap little lighted marquee that reads, BEST FOOD IN TOWN, a claim that cannot possibly be true, but nobody begrudges Red bragging rights to running the toughest food joint in town. A tough town.

Step down five steps between two dark doors. *Sauza's 2.75 cuz it's happy hour.*

Sexy posters and paintings above the bar. I sat beneath a seminude brunette wearing only a sheer blue veil that draped loosely from her forearms and stretched taut over her ass. There was also a thrilling pencil drawing of Angelina Jolie, but beside her the cartoonish blonde surrounded by classic cars was not sexy at all.

Sunshine arrived and ordered a Manhattan. The only thing calling itself scotch at Red's was Johnnie Walker, so I scanned the bourbons instead and chose Maker's Mark. The restaurant crowded up around us and our drinks came.

Sunshine snorted back his Manhattan and popped the cherry in his mouth. "Can I get another one of these?" he called to the bartender. When he leaned into me I got a heavy whiff of marijuana smoke on his greasy flower-print shirt. "How the fuck did you get out there to the

Johnson house? What the fuck were you doing way the fuck out in Ledoux?"

I wasn't sure how to say it without sounding like an asshole. "Chasing some tail."

The moment I said it I regretted it. Here I was confessing to a burnt-out hippie something I wouldn't want my wife to find out. Of course, he would never have a way of telling her, but I regretted letting him in on my secret all the same.

"Bullshit."

"I thought this girl was coming on to me. She said she and her friends partied out there."

"Did she show up?"

"No." I decided it would be best to change course. "Look, there's someone I know who I believe might be a mutual acquaintance. Name's Mel Woburn. He told me you lived there. I would just like to find out what it was like, and then I'll never bother you again."

Sunshine, Shorn, Harold—whatever—looked at me with a beery eye. "The hippies never owned the place, but we added the log room and built the portal. Bad shit happened around that place. Mel probably told you. Even regular shit would spin out of control."

"What kind of regular shit?"

Sunshine looked at me vacantly for a moment, then his fresh drink came and he became reanimated. "Mel mentioned Ritchie Motherfucker, right?"

"Yup."

"Him and his old lady slept in the last room, the furthest adobe from the log room. Did you look in there?"

"The last room was padlocked."

Sunshine nodded effusively, hit his drink. "The day

Ritchie fell off a horse he said, *I'm okay.* A minor fracture, right? Just lay up in bed for a while. But a week later he was dead of sepsis. He didn't want to go to no doctor. Said, *I'm treating it with goldenseal.* Ritchie and his fucking goldenseal!"

Red's was starting to serve lunch. Big plates heaped with steaming steaks kept coming out of the kitchen. Sunshine grabbed a passing waitress by her bicep, subduing her. A strange glaze came over her eyes; she knew a lifetime of abusive men and how to keep them at bay by behaving docile.

"Can you get me one of those lunch specials, honey?" Sunshine said.

She said, "Coming right up."

Sunshine drank deeply and we ordered him another. He wiped his mouth on his sleeve and looked at me. We were drinking lunch together, and I was buying. Sing for my meal, said his expression. The Manhattans started making their magic, and Sunshine let me have it.

"That gangrene moved fucking fast," he said, "and the fever made Ritchie incoherent. We finally decided we had to get him down to Mora, and we loaded him in the station wagon, but the rains were so bad it took us all day. By the time we got to the hospital it was too late. He was dead.

"The admitting nurse said she'd do us a favor, save us fifty bucks by shredding up the file and un-admitting him, but then it would be up to us to remove the body and contact the county coroner. *Remove the body?* This was Ritchie! Just the other day we were riding horses together. But that's where it was at and so we did what we had to do. We put the seats down in the back of the station wagon and drove him back out to the Johnson house.

"It took a long time to get him to burn, a lot of gasoline, and he stunk like hell, that hairy bastard! Shit, we should have had the girls shave him, but it was too late, he was already smoldering up, so we poured on more gasoline and sent the girls for more sticks. It was a good thing we sent them away because of what happened next."

"What?"

"He got up."

"*What?*"

"Ritchie: dead Ritchie. Got up right there. One of those nerve things you read about, but it went on and on. He was running around the yard, hit some bushes and set them on fire and just kept going.

"I looked at Little Joe and we both had these awful faces. Do we tackle him or what? Run away? Little Joe went for the hose. Ritchie finally fell to the ground and started rolling around, groaning. I got pretty close but then I shrank back at what I saw: Ritchie's face, his expression of torture and melting beard and charred skin, but it was Ritchie's face, and he was looking at me in anguish, Ritchie, his feet already in hell."

"What did you do?"

Sunshine's plate came. He carved off a forkful of steak, talking over the chewing. "We had to shoot him."

"Jesus . . ."

"Then Little Joe hit him with a jet from the hose and Ritchie curled up just like a dead bug. God, that was awful, that smell, and the vomit, mine and Little Joe's. The girls came back screaming *What happened?* before they saw it and vomited too. After that, we couldn't get him lighted again."

Sunshine pitched another forkful of steak into his mouth.

"The weird shit started long before the hippies ever got there. Back in the 1800s Johnson's son killed his mom and sisters, and then he hanged himself—the whole fucking family except for old man Johnson." He threw back the last of his drink and stood. "I got to take a piss."

The bill came and I pulled out my wallet. I handed the waitress my check card.

Out in the blazing parking lot, I asked him, "How long did the hippies live there?"

Climbing into his Volkswagen van, Sunshine said, "Place finally shut down in '74. Last I heard some bikers set up a lab in the end room and made meth."

Something clicked at that instant. The place had been a meth lab. I had read an article on how motel rooms have to be stripped of all furniture and sometimes even re-Sheetrocked after they've been contaminated with meth-making chemicals.

I sat in the Spider and considered my options. I was already down in the valley. I could make it over the mountains in about two hours. The afternoon was wide open.

What was it about the Johnson house that kept calling me back? At first I just wanted to see. What did I expect to see? I wanted to see it in daytime. It had taken away my camera, my computer, but it had given me a story.

After the laptop, I should have just let it go. The crash of the Mac might have been a blessing in disguise: begin with a clean slate, and not only that, begin with a new slate, a different slate.

I took out the Altoids tin, lit a joint, and set out north on 68 toward Mora.

On the Fourth of July I had sped hornily to my goal without taking an account of my surroundings, but now I made note of all the towns along the way.

Española: a woman from Spain once ran the only tavern here, an outpost on the Camino Real halfway between Taos and Santa Fe.

Alcalde: "the mayor," the first occupation of the Spanish empire on future U.S. soil. I avoided the package store at Marcy Garcia's Club Lumina, suicide for a white boy like me, but stopped for a beer at the Shamrock in Velarde.

Embudo: the funnel between these foothills of the Sangre de Cristo. I navigated the curves of the canyon with a twenty-four-ounce Chelada between my knees, turning right at the winery.

In Dixon, La Chiripada, a stroke of good fortune: an *Open* sign on Sunday! I stopped for a tasting. The son of the founders hit my glass hard: reds, whites, a brandy-fortified wine. I left braced for the winding road into the mountains.

Peñasco: "the rocky place," where I ditched the empty Chelada can at the drive-in trash barrel.

Through Sipapu, the Swiss village, and over the pass.

Mora: depending on whom you asked, it could be a patronymic, but there was also a legend of a French trapper hunting pelts along the river, who came upon a dead man facedown on the shore. He was a young man and, other than being dead, appeared to be in good health. There had been no signs of struggle, no injuries whatsoever on the body. The trapper dug the unfortunate man a shallow grave in the sand of the riverbank and forsook that place in a hurry, leaving it with a designation, *L'eau de mort*, that lingers two hundred years later. Mora.

At the Mustang I paid at the pump and took a piss inside. I thought about another Chelada, but I needed to wake up a little for the drive into Ledoux, so got myself a hot coffee instead.

I wanted to find the dirt road direct to the house so I wouldn't have to climb the hill from Morphy Lake. I drove for more than an hour before spotting the sign for Aplanado.

It looked almost like a driveway, unmarked, but at the turn it skirted between two fenced properties and up the back of a wooded slope. It was one of those roads that had never been planned and so from its origins had remained neglected.

I met no other vehicles or people on the narrow one-track. Barely broad enough for a single car, Aplanado would never be widened, paved, or even so much as graded. There were too many gnarly old trees and boulders on either side.

A little more than a mile into the woods, the road came out of the trees and the valley opened up: the distant peaks, their age-beaten granite faces reminding me of the harsh winters that punish the green valley at eight thousand feet.

The hump of a culvert, a bend in the road, and I

passed the gate I had hopped over on the Fourth of July. I had to drive the dirt road another quarter-mile to find a spot wide enough to turn the Spider back around.

I pulled off into the tall grass at the edge of the property line. When I cut the engine there was only the din of crickets and grasshoppers. I checked my phone: no service.

I walked to the gate. At the end of the drive hung a rusted metal sign I hadn't seen in the dark, a cedar shingle nailed eight feet up in a tree, the Spanish lettering painted in decorative script. It said something like, *For the favor of not trespassing, we will not have to shoot you.*

I had the feeling that there was nobody else alive in the wide valley. There was no other house, not a sign of life, not even a distant buzz of chainsaw in the hot afternoon.

Now that I had invested the energy in coming back, I felt there was something at stake. I would hear anyone coming. I climbed over the gate.

I approached slowly around the side of the house. Six posts on a wooden portal.

I looked around in the bushes but I didn't find Oppie's bag of bones. Maybe some other dog had dragged them off.

I stepped onto the portal and stood in the black doorway. Bad shit had happened here.

When my eyes adjusted I stepped inside onto the trash-strewn floor. Who had been the last occupants? Why had they left in such a hurry? The ruin of the mattress was there in the first room. What would make me lie down on that filthy bed? Nothing.

When I crossed the threshold and walked out in

the middle of the floor, over my shoulder came a loud squeaking like the sound of an old bicycle.

I stood stiffly in place. What am I doing? This isn't a game. I'm trespassing. Someone might take this seriously, some insane or homeless person. Just because a house is abandoned doesn't mean that it's unoccupied.

I was ready to look over my shoulder and see a deranged old hippie or angry Hispanic twirling a rusty chain crank, ready to hit me with it, but when I turned the room was empty except for the trash on the floor.

The squeaking abruptly stopped, and the interval of silence allowed me to briefly collect my senses. I took a step and the sound came again from the ceiling. I saw a clod of mud and straw suspended from a viga in the center of the room.

I stepped closer. The sound hadn't been squeaking; it was chirping.

I stood under the nest, holding my hand up to block the light from the entrance. Three little beaks peeked out: three blind baby swallows. When I passed in front of the window, my shadow fell over the mouth of the nest and the chicks thought their mother was home.

I felt penetrated by exhaustion, a narcotic fatigue. The sunlight and sound of grasshoppers flooded in every window, suffusing the room with soporific warmth.

The laptop, the camera, Kitty's cruelty—none of it bothered me now. I felt good. It was such a quiet valley, such a dozy afternoon. I had not slept more than a couple of hours each of the past three nights.

I lay on the floor to rest my eyes.

* * *

In the dream my father showed up—my father as he was at forty, when I was still a boy, before he went to Fair Oaks.

I heard myself speak. *What are you doing here?*

I kept coming here too. I couldn't help it. One taste and I was hooked.

That's impossible. You never in your life got out of the Northeast. For the last five years you never left Fair Oaks. Whatever remains of you lies in St. Theresa's Catholic Cemetery along the cold clays of the Passaic.

He gave me a loving smile and said, *We all come here eventually. That's why it feels so familiar. But when you go in the last room and try telling anyone about what you saw, they shut you up, they call you crazy, they try to lock you up. They can't face it.*

My father kneeled and placed a hand on the back of my head, gently stroking my hair like he used to in the night when I was a little boy. Then something made him look over my shoulder. *Here comes,* he said. My father exited the dream, and when I turned and peered through the window, I saw a great cloud of ash and smoke rising over the mountains.

I woke in a panic. From the darkness beneath a broken plank of flooring, a pair of rodent eyes stared at me.

I scrambled to my hands and knees. The mouse disappeared beneath the house. Jesus, Oberhelm, what has become of you? You are a wreck sprawled on the floor of a dirty old house.

Out the window I could see the beautiful mountains, the tops of the pines glowing green-gold in the afternoon sun. No smoke.

I had to get out of there. The trill of a cricket stuck in the room with me drowned out all other sound.

I looked at the padlocked door. Before I left, I wanted to see in that last room.

I headed out to the Spider and reached under the seat for the tire iron, and then I went back in the house to the padlocked door.

I slipped the tire iron in the gap behind the hinge that held the lock in place. I leaned on it a little and the hinge snapped off, splintering the rotten doorframe.

When I opened the door, cold air sucked me in with a gasp. The one window to the outside had been bricked up. The only light inside came in with me. There were three plain mud walls and one covered with paper; otherwise there was only a rustic table where someone had left a book. Bound in black vellum: the Bible.

I flicked my lighter and flipped through the pages. On the back I found an inscription in black ink: *Draw on the power of these mouldering pages to finishe what we started.*

Nice word choice. They'd gotten the feel right: moldering meant rotting, and spelling it with the extra vowel made it sound even mealier: mould. Like mold in your mouth. And "finish" with an e? Like olde Englishe?

What had made someone write this in the back of the Bible? Hard to tell what it meant. I left it on the table where I'd found it.

I looked at the wall that was papered, pages torn from a magazine stuck to the crumbling plaster.

I flicked my lighter again and saw something familiar in the typeface, the layout: high-quality photos and plenty of white space to set off the meager sustenance of the story. The words looked familiar.

That's when I saw. A thing in the lettering drew my eyes.

Those are my words. I wrote those stories. They are pages torn from *Surge*. My name stands out at the top of every page.

I pulled into the Mustang parking lot and bought a four-pack of Kahlua Mudslides. Then I got back in the car, shook up a Mudslide, and opened it. I sat in the Spider and drank.

The taste of the sugar and milk solids gave my heart a lift, and then easing the jitters came the Kahlua and the vodka. Was it really even vodka? I checked the label: *Contains Real Vodka!* I felt better already.

Why would my articles be on the wall of that house?

I removed the other three Mudslides from the carton, turned the cardboard inside out, and found a pen in the glove compartment to work my way through the names and associations.

Sunshine
didn't know me before today
doesn't want anything to do with the house

Mel Woburn
weak connection with the house
six years pot dealer

Blood tech
got me out there in the first place
didn't show up

I had left the pages hanging on the wall, part afraid

to touch them, part afraid of what would happen in my head if I admitted I was afraid to leave them there. It would be an acknowledgment that I suspected this had been deliberate, something depraved.

Two Mudslides down and I started to relax. Copies of *Surge*, bundles of them, get dumped all over northern New Mexico like so many *Thrifty Nickels*. Someone just tore a few up and tacked those pages to the ugly mud wall to cover it. Ridiculous to think of it as anything more than a coincidence. I live over the mountain in Los Alamos—just drive away.

Ready to get back on the road, I opened another Mudslide and pulled out of the Mustang parking lot.

When I got back to Los Alamos it was going on dark, and I found a note Kitty had written in the kitchen. *Where the fuck have you been???* At the top of the stairs, the bedroom door was closed. I listened. Oppie did not get up and I did not bother going in.

I went down to my study, rolled a joint, and woke up the PC.

Googling *Mora* and *Johnson massacre* got me nothing, and *New Mexico* plus *Johnson House* yielded thousands of hits, but nothing on the first page more relevant than the newspaper headline, *Johnson: House Stays on Schedule*.

What if I looked up the owner in county files? Resources sucked online, and even if I made the special trip to Mora it might not lead to anything worthwhile. There were thousands of absentee owners in these valleys.

Sometimes it was because the grandparents willed the house to kids or grandkids they never saw in Albuquerque, and Albuquerque changed people. They might say, *Oh, I've got a beautiful patch of land up in Mora County I'm going to retire on and farm someday.* But someday never came because the SUVs, the Cottonwood Mall, and the fast food on Central Avenue was the way they really wanted to live.

Sometimes it was because the titular owner was someone up the valley in a McMansion who wanted a pristine view of an old adobe without any junk cars on it and without any redneck renter shooting guns and running four-wheelers.

Sometimes the entitled were distant relatives of the former owners, heirs who barely knew they owned a place in the middle of nowhere—sometimes they didn't know they owned a place at all.

I got on LexisNexis and the Lab's username and password autofilled. Straight to WorldCat, search entries containing *Johnson* and *Mora* and *New Mexico*, and limit results by publication date before 1900. I got a hit with full text online: *Mora marriages, births & deaths: Book no. 1, February 4, 1856, to December 1875; authors: Padilla y Baca, Luis Gilberto.*

I searched the text for *Johnson*, and there he was on Aplanado Road: J. Johnson. In 1860 he married Maria Montoya. She gave birth to children listed in the registry as *male, 1861; fem., 1865; fem., 1872.*

The deaths of the mother, the son, and the two girls were all recorded as 1874. That would have made the son only thirteen years old.

There was no death recorded for Mr. Johnson, at least not by 1875. I searched again to see if I could find a *Book no. 2,* but I got *No documents found matching your request.*

Book no. 1 was the only volume available online.

Could a thirteen-year-old have done something like that? Maybe the contemporaneous deaths had been caused by disease.

OCLC FirstSearch. Votre session est terminée.

The sky was lightening in the east. Shivering under the effect of the Mudslides and the bourbon, I lay down on the living room couch.

My nightmare did not begin right away. It came on gradually like a virus. Maybe if I looked closely I would have seen that milder symptoms had already set in. Or maybe if I had never gone back to the house, the nightmare would never have started in the first place.

It happened more than a hundred winters ago, when the snow got above the roofline. The month of January 1874, the average temperature 14 degrees Fahrenheit. The high 21 degrees, and the lowest recorded -23. The snow down in the valley had measured 84 inches. It's hard to imagine what the snowdrifts of Ledoux had made of a baseline seven feet of snow.

You come to this valley to farm. The land is good and cheap for a homesteader, and if the Spanish people didn't understand you, all the better that they should leave you alone. Idle associations and casual conversations lead to blasphemous speech, sinful ruminations, and evil actions. It is good when you arrive with your family in the spring and good to work hard and be outside all day in the summer. Just gathering wood goes on hours after dark on moonlit nights, and you come home so exhausted there is barely energy for the meal and Bible study before the onset of a sleep like death. Then, with the first light of dawn and the rooster's strangled cry, back to work.

Autumn brings the harvest and opportunities to instill with prayer and instruction the knowledge that rewards are not from our labor alone but for the glory of God. The more His favor was upon us, the more we needed to pray. Sometimes for hours in the dark, and if one is caught dropping off, you have a willow switch with which to administer penance to the flesh that God might spare their souls.

Winter is all that you did not foresee. The days are too cold to work the earth. There is only so much wood to split. And the nights are long, and even with prayer petitioning blessings in the spring there are still many idle hours to fill between sleep. The Spanish families fill them with card games, marble tournaments, and telling legends from their wicked folklore—idolatries, blasphemies. You will not let your children fall into such corruption. If you had been able to look at it clearly—if your brother in town had been able to see you—you might have realized that which torments you is not the soul and the spirit, but a variant of cabin fever. Instead, you enforce a code of silence among family in the winter. You do not believe in idle talk. The only book you keep in the house is the Bible. Deciding that speech is the inception of vice, you forbid speaking altogether.

You impose a strict code of silence among your wife and three children—a son, a young daughter, and a baby girl. You had better eat right in the Johnson house, because even a rumble of the stomach adds up against you on the way to a beating. The house becomes a tomb. No sniffling, hiccupping, or sighing. You catch a cold, you go out to the barn to cough.

The wind ducts in from the chimney, and it howls down to the floor in the corner where the boy sleeps with the dusty blanket his mother knit for him from churro wool. He looks up at the mica pane that serves as the family's only window—covered with snow.

It is one room, no portal. Although the isolation makes days terrible, the nights are still worse: fourteen-hour stretches of pitch darkness beside tepid coals. You forbid burning wood at night when the mother isn't cooking and everyone has their cobijas. The boy can hear his brother and sister breathing, but they cannot steal glances to console each other. These fleeting glimpses of humanity are all that keep him from slipping into the trap of forgetting that he is not your slave, that the world is not his father's dominion. This is what you want them to believe. This is how you control them.

You stand up and look at the son. You have to milk the heifer, and you communicate as much by picking up the bucket and shovel before going to the door and putting on your high boots. Her udders are swollen, and soon this will make her sick.

You have to clear the path of snow out the front door. The last snow blocked the slab of micaceous rock that served as the one window. The weight of it caused the roof to collapse in places.

It is like digging out fresh. You use the milk bucket to carry loads of snow to the end of the path where the small barn has a low portal in front of the door.

The son takes turns shoveling.

58 steps to the barn door. The howling wind.

You look at your son, thirteen years old, so he knows what has to be done. Your look says: You take care of the family.

The first to go was the mother, a shrewd choice on the son's part as she was the only one who might have overcome him. It took a lot of swings as he got used to wielding the heavy ax-head at this angle, when before he brought it over his head to split logs on a charred stump. Her hands were hacked to pieces by the time he delivered the crushing blow to her cranium. Just like splitting wood. And then he went to his sister who waited in the door. Only the baby succeeded in letting out a scream.

You get back and find it. Flesh of my flesh, blood of my blood. The baby rests in the mother's arms, both of them bloody. Your daughter is there, her fingers strewn on the floor. The stumps that remain on the wrists are black and swollen. One overhead blow had cleaved her skull. You look up at your son, look up at the viga with the knot. Counting from the door, the boy had hanged himself from the third one.

You sit in the room with them. Nobody farting or sniffing. Nobody's lungs drawing a breath and nobody's blood coursing through veins. It is finally quiet. You think of the last thing you said. You take care of the family.

I stood at the bathroom mirror, my hand throbbing. Kitty called groggily from bed: "Drop Oppie at Salon des Chiens." It was the first thing she had said to me since we got back from camping, and I understood what she was talking about. Oppie's fur was still full of burrs and goat heads from the camping trip.

I unloaded my golf bag while Oppie jumped playfully in and out of the trunk. "Down, boy!" When I lay the towel out on the passenger seat of the Spider, he hopped in and curled up like a little gentleman, careful to keep his claws away from the leather back.

I took off Oppie's house collar, the nice phrase Kitty used to describe the shocker, and put on the travel collar. When I would open the garage door, Oppie would sometimes bolt after a jogger, but with a little jolt from the invisible fence system, he'd pull up short of the sidewalk.

It was a bright summer morning on the Hill. I pulled the Spider out of the garage and made the drive to Trinity. The bank clock flashed *7:45 / 80°*. Jesus!

I put the top down on the Spider with the switch. Hundreds of people were already downtown driving their big cars and walking on wide, clean sidewalks. "Wait here," I told Oppie, ducking into Starbucks.

The same faces as always greeted me from behind the counter: hard-working people from the valley who got up in the dark and took buses or drove from fifty miles away to prepare the food for the people who live on the Hill.

I crowded up to the counter amongst those they served, well-dressed people with healthy-looking skin and serene smiles that hinted at substantial assets. We were taking advantage of the time before work to get our morning sweets, little treats that would make the day go by. This was the demographic that had weathered the recent recession without need for concern, most of them millionaires who can't and aren't allowed to explain what it is they work on, who don't want to know my name, just good morning, nice day, see you tomorrow, for the next thirty-five years or so.

While the sun beat in through the windows of the café on a scorching summer morning, I had a brief flash of satisfaction. These are your subjects: the sources of your profiles, puff pieces you pen for *Surge*, but also subjects of your rule, because don't you, in ways that matter to many of them more than who is head of the DOE or even president, determine their destinies, frame their fates, and tell their stories in the place that most counts—this insular community of scientists?

I walked back out to the Spider and gave Oppie the cheese from my breakfast panini. He gulped it down before knowing what hit him.

At eight o'clock I pulled into the parking lot at Le Salon des Chiens and put Oppie on the leash. In the reception area I overheard a woman tell the girl at the counter, "Harvey said, *No kids, my career is our kid*, so he got me this dog." There was no irony in the woman's voice, a Prozac vacancy to her eyes, and no apologies for the little blue coat on her pet.

Kitty, too, was becoming like this. I would hear her on the phone with friends: *You're never going to believe what Oppie did today.*

I handed the leash to the grooming assistant. "All right, Op. Your mom will be here by ten."

When I got to the Lab, the closest parking space I could find was about a half-mile from my office. I would get in my ten to twenty minutes of aerobic exercise today. I took my briefcase and my skinny latte.

In the foyer I put my hand on the ID screen and the door opened to the offices of *Surge*. It had excessive security for an employee magazine that published nothing other than fluff, but my building had once housed a classified division, and palm-reader screens were SOP for the Lab.

I said good morning to Golz and asked how her long weekend was.

"Not as long as yours," she accurately observed. "MQR for you."

Golz is sexy in a skinny, spinsterish (even though she is supposedly married) sort of way. I remember coming in sweating for the interview because I hadn't known it was going to be such a hike from the parking lot. The way Golz studied me across the conference table, large enough to seat eight without elbows touching, I could tell I was a finalist. I had tasted salt on my lips, along with the word *salary*, but I would not say it. That time would come. The office was air-conditioned, but not the kind that throws you into shivers. It was just Golz in her red wool, Hillary-wannabe skirt suit and me in my coat and tie around a big conference table. What was Golz wondering about me? I knew: can this guy deliver decent copy, keep his nose clean, preserve reasonably chemical-free blood, and not fall from grace with the added factor of classification, clearance, and keeping an eye out for breaches that was known organizationally as SAP?

Security Awareness Protocol, they call it, and everyone who works for the Lab has to follow SAP. Like everyone else on the Hill, I have gone through the training, and like everyone I have been subjected to clandestine checkups at stores, the supermarket, restaurants—these are little tests SAP gives you, from a stylish dinner party where you realize a guest is baiting everyone to ask him about his division, to a clever rendering of the clueless fellow at the home-improvement store asking, *Excuse me, do you happen to know what kind of parts I need to make a detonator?*

If I was always a little scornful of the goons at SAP, it's not because I thought their jobs weren't important. It was their lack of style that bugged me: a weak broth of McCarthyist paranoia and patriotic posturing. Why couldn't they get a real writer on their staff to add some flair to their reports and memoranda? The answer was self-evident: a talented writer would have to lobotomize himself just to get in the door. It was all about FOUO and an aesthetic they had probably ripped off from a Renaissance fair. Their logo was actually a purple dragon!

I went into my office, logged on to my cleared computer, and checked my inbox. Besides writing profiles for the print version of *Surge*, I reworked SAP's jumbled press releases, translating them into standard English for the *Surge* feed, and Golz had e-mailed me an MQR—mandatory quarterly reminder—for SAP's online schedule of espionage-awareness classes:

SAP Week at the Laboratory is geared to raise awareness or instruct employees on counterintelligence and counterterrorism with a series of talks or seminars that instruct employees on what to guard against when traveling abroad, and the basics of counterintelligence and how you can be targeted by people unless you are aware of the possibilities. And other classes on electronic spying and terrorism.

What a train wreck! I loved the juxtaposition of that first run-on sentence with the last fragment, vagaries like *talks or seminars*, and that pearl of passive-voice construction: *how you can be targeted by people.*

I couldn't complain. The fact that national-security wonks can't write kept me well fed. To make it tweetable, I turned the copy into haiku. I typed:

Traveling abroad?
Unless you learn how spies think,
they could target you.

Take a SAP Week class
in online espionage
or terrorism.

Chuckling (always chuckling) privately (always privately), *And for this you get 125k and bennies*, I bounced the revised MQR brief back to Golz and asked her to declassify it so I could post it to the feed.

Although I had my own login and password with complete publishing rights on the blog, Communications Protocol insisted on this precaution as a CYA, and I always sent even the most basic post to Golz for declassification.

Golz was my favorite kind of editor: she who does not write. She never changes what you write, but she ultimately has to answer for what gets written.

Within minutes Golz replied with a *Declassify*, and the post went out.

Besides proofing the blog and keeping it readable, I wrote four or five short features a month on retired scientists' hobbies and recreational interests for the glossy print edition of *Surge*. My copy workload added up to about 1,500 words a week. That left a lot of time between profiles for scenic drives and rounds of golf.

Profile struck me as an apt word for these pieces, designed to show only one side of the subjects' faces. *Klein grows gigantic green chile in his backyard vegetable garden. Saporov catches a prize-winning trout at Abiquiu Lake.*

What they did at their jobs I couldn't ask. "Get a feel for your subjects," said Golz, "light features. Nothing classified." If during Q&A I got too close to the bone of what one of my subjects was actually working on, I'd get the L.A. glaze and faraway eyes.

A few of them might admit to being physicists, but I wasn't even allowed to ask specialty—e.g., theoretical or particle physics? That's life in Los Alamos. That's security awareness. That's SAP. And *Surge*, with its slick production and trendy design, was just a vanity sheet to stroke the scientists' egos.

The print run was in the thousands, but we didn't have to sell advertising. It didn't matter whether anyone off the Hill read *Surge*. The intended audience wasn't necessarily even other employees at the Lab. The real target was the subject of the profile himself.

Golz and I never spoke openly about it, but we both knew my job and the role of *Surge* was to placate all of the pseudofamous geezers with a feature spread, if not a cover, before they were too old or too dead. If you write about them in their little rag in their artificial world on the Hill, maybe they won't go around looking for attention in the real world of journalism, the world of conspiracy theorists, spies, and identity thieves.

My subjects wanted to see their stories in print. *I want people to know my name*, they thought as much as anyone else with their talents, *but I can't talk to anybody outside my division about what I really do. Nobody can know what I'm really known for, so out of necessity I cultivate an odd hobby, a decoy accomplishment, a small masterwork of gardening, gadgetry, or gizmo collecting, in order to get a bit of print recognition in my lifetime.*

I put the finishing touches on a profile of a famous physicist, eighty-nine-year-old Barney Marcosi, and his interest in fly-fishing. We had spoken about his fly collection. The August issue was about to get put to bed, and I wrote three one-sentence captions for the photos Golz had chosen to accompany the profile.

I jotted a few shorthand notes for the questions I would ask my 10:30 subject, and then I got on my computer and searched the collection at the Lab's library for *Mora, New Mexico*. Nothing, but that wasn't surprising. The Lab's library is pure science, a "National Research" library on physics and aeronautics.

I got on the Los Alamos Mesa Public Library catalog and found a small-press book about Mora titled *Valley of the Witches*. I sent the call numbers to my phone and

left the office at 10:15, informing Golz over my shoulder,
"Interview."

I brought a pen and an empty notebook and walked a brisk half-mile back across the parking lot to the Spider. Although I always typed drafts of my profiles on the office computer, I still preferred pen and paper for interview notes. It set most subjects at ease better than a geek wielding a laptop or tablet between them, and there is no substitute for blank paper when literally drawing connections between topics and themes. Besides, I like to cross my legs when sitting for an interview. Try typing on crossed legs.

I parked in the shade of a cottonwood in front of the residence of my subject: Harumi Ogawa, a Japanese physicist famous in the field of systems analysis. The week before I had requested a brief from Operations Protocol. I reread it now on my phone:

Chief Criticality Officer from 1945 until his retirement in 1983, now 94 years old. Cannot easily walk or stand. His wife, 20 years younger, helps him get comfortable before guests are admitted. Hobby: microminiatures. N.B.: Do NOT raise the subject of the criticality accidents.

As chief criticality officer, Ogawa's job had been preventing the occurrence of a criticality accident, which was a pretty way of saying someone, while conducting an experiment, catching a fatal dose of radiation. For four decades, his record promoting safety at the labs had been almost impeccable, except for two early accidents involving a radioactive sphere that had earned the nickname Demon Core. I knew the story from all the Los Alamos history books: a fourteen-pound, melon-sized ball of plutonium had gone supercritical in two separate freak accidents in 1945 and 1946.

Harry Daghlian worked alone on August 21, 1945, just days after Hiroshima and Nagasaki. He hovered over a nickel-plated plutonium sphere weighing 6.2 kilograms. The sphere had not yet been dubbed the Demon Core.

Daghlian took several tungsten-carbide blocks and stacked them around the plutonium sphere. He moved a block to take a measurement and dropped it accidentally into the center of the assembly. It touched the sphere. There was a superprompt—that is, micromomentary—spike in the neutron population: radiation, heat, and finally a blue flash when the air became ionized around the neutron burst. His hand shot out in reflex to remove the dropped block, but he was flashed by a radioactive dose estimated at 510 rem. He suffered acute radiation poisoning, and four weeks later he was dead.

The following year, a scientist named Louis Slotin held a screwdriver between two half-spheres of beryllium and the same core. It slipped and the core went supercritical. The radiation killed him nine days later.

Operations Protocol said this topic was off-limits, so unless Ogawa brought it up I would stick to his hobby. For leisure, Ogawa had engineered the fabrication of atom-sized sculptures, most recently a microscopic noodle bowl with chopsticks just two atoms thick.

Ogawa's wife showed me into the living room. Along

with my notebook I carried a bag emblazoned with the CB Fox logo.

Ogawa was waiting in his chair with his hands folded on his lap, no newspaper or open book. He gazed benignly while I performed an informal bow, back straight and hands at my sides. Ogawa nodded slightly. His wife bowed and backed out of the room.

I put down my notebook and opened the bag, took out a gift box, and lay it on a footstool before Ogawa. "*Ohayō gozaimasu* . . . it only amounts to a symbol of my appreciation, but . . ."

Ogawa opened the box. Inside were alloy salt and pepper shakers from Nambé designs. "Thank you. They are very stylish." Ogawa's wife reappeared to take the shaker set away.

Ogawa offered a little boxed gift as well. From the size and weight, I guessed it was a folding fan or a set of serving spoons.

"You should not have gone through the trouble."

"It is just a little something, nothing much."

"Thank you, Harumi-san." Ogawa did not ask me to open the box, so I observed etiquette by laying his gift aside quietly to open later.

"You have traveled in Japan?" he asked.

"I have never had the privilege."

In fact, I had merely Googled Japanese custom and spent ten minutes on Wikipedia.

"Then you have worked or lived among Japanese here?"

I smiled and gave a half-nod so as not to contradict the venerable scientist. I could mention the freshman-year roommate from Japan, but that might lead to questions of where, and to be honest I had never found out. He had been a bookworm and computer nerd and we rarely spoke to each other much less spent time together, although he once helped me through a nasty hangover by fixing up some strong black tea.

I took out my pen. "Dr. Ogawa, please tell me about your incredible noodle bowl."

We had a long conversation during which the questions I had prepared wove naturally through a weft of pleasant solicitude. I obligingly played the familiar part of the fawning graduate student, volleying Ogawa's anecdotes with exclamations like "Interesting," "Fascinating," "Amazing," and all the time taking notes, nodding, squinting with an intensity that said, *Your story—your cleared story—means something to me, to the people who will read it in the magazine.*

Ogawa's wife served hot green tea and he mused on the team at the Tokyo University of Agriculture and Technology that had extracted gasoline from pressurized cow dung.

I sipped my tea and found my mind wandering: a spike of light shooting from my chest . . . a dog dragging a bag of bones out of the woods . . . I recovered from my brief distraction and realized Ogawa was looking at me, waiting for the next question.

I went to stock: "What book have you recently read that impressed you?"

"Ah, have you read Murakami's *Underground*?"

"Yes, I know the book—about the 1995 sarin attacks on the Tokyo subway."

"Yes, sarin—here is a gas twenty-six times more deadly than cyanide. The pain in the eyes and lungs must have been terrible in the subway cars, and yet the passengers did not talk to each other to acknowledge their rising discomfort until the pain had become almost unbearable."

Ogawa drank his tea in three steady gulps. He put down the cup, paused with eyes shut, and said, "Now, let me tell you about the Demon Core."

I leaned forward, my expression impassive. Ogawa had brought it on himself.

He sighed, motioning at the mantel where he kept some of his medals. "You are familiar with the object?"

"Certainly." I gave Ogawa the worried frown, the pursed lips, the sympathetic-puppy look of the interviewer-confessor. "But I would be grateful for your story."

Ogawa nodded and peered into the near-empty cup as if to divine from the leaves a best means of inception, but how to speak of the unspeakable? There is no good way to recount a great horror.

Ogawa closed his eyes and said, "I wish to tell you something I have told nobody. When I heard how the first man touched the brick to the core, I thought I had failed to account for something, anything, which might have been foreseen to prevent such an event. But the second man with the screwdriver—I realized there is no such thing as prevention." He looked somewhere back in his skull. "I have often wondered: what is it that draws men to self-destruction?"

"What they call 'tickling the tail of the dragon'?"

Ogawa shook his head and fluttered his hand in the air to wave this jargon away. "I do not mean suicide, or tempting fate by flirting with danger. Something more

complex. It is the power of what this man is holding—
something so small that can be so destructive. He perhaps
doubts it could be true. He forgets his physicality."

I finished taking notes quietly, closed the notebook,
and said, "I am grateful, Harumi-san, for the fascinating interview. I will of course courier you a draft of the
layout to approve all quotations attributed to you before
publication."

He made a slight gesture to rise. I stood and bowed.

Not bad, that last part, and an exclusive too. I
wouldn't use it in *Surge*. I would save it for a commis-
sioned piece in the mainstream press someday, maybe
an obituary. Enough major articles in national periodi-
cals, and I'd collect the best in a book, a memoir of a
cub in Los Alamos. I'd tell how much I learned about the
range of human characters from authoring these biopics
of mad scientists.

Never befriend them. It was death to befriend them.
Just like high-profile journalists or certain expensive
shrinks, there was the serious risk of getting stuck with
a stalker, a subject who says to himself: you coaxed out
my story, you gave me fifteen minutes in the spotlight,
you seemed to care, and now I'm going to keep telling
you every time I finish another needlepoint (I'm really
making strides in my art!) or when the peppers yield
an incredible crop (my thumb is even greener than I
thought!).

Get the story and get out of there before the coffee
is cold. Golz would rebuff the *how-ya-doin?* follow-ups. I
gave her a little shortlist of excuses to lob at callers at
random: he's at a conference, in an all-day meeting, on
assignment on an atoll. Never befriend them, and yet

leave them feeling like they made a friend—one they'd never see again.

It was high noon and scorching hot outside. I got back to the car and tossed Ogawa's box on the passenger seat. Then I thought about it again before starting the car and opened the top of the box. It was a pen—a really nice pen—a Parker, ballpoint, but with a space-age nib and a streamline stem. I slipped it in my breast pocket and drove back to town.

I didn't feel like returning to the office, so I stopped at the Mesa Public Library to check out the book on Mora and to take a piss after the long interview and all the green tea.

Someone had Sharpied on the tile above my urinal: NAZIS. Nice. Every once in a while some old-timer making a pit stop here must get really shook up seeing that accusation in midstream.

I made a swing through the New Mexico history aisle and found the book on Mora, *Valley of the Witches*, a hand-bound manuscript that looked like it had been put together at a copy shop. I stopped by the checkout and gave the librarian my card to scan.

Out in the blistering-hot parking lot I threw the book in the backseat of the Spider and swung by Smith's on the way home to get myself a half-pint of Jägermeister for a bracer.

I walked into the kitchen and found Kitty talking with one of the ladies from her women's group. The friend—what was her name? Alina, Adelina, Analina?—cut me a look like, *You monster*.

"What?" I said. They immediately fell silent.

Kitty wanted to have a talk about the dog. Oppie had been brooding all day since she had picked him up from his haircut. "When you dropped him off in the morning, you didn't achieve adequate closure."

"Not this again."

"Lars says you have to say *See you soon* instead of *Goodbye*, and tell him who will be picking him up and in approximately how long." Fucking Lars, the pet psychic I'd never met but who I could already tell Kitty wanted to fuck—if they weren't already fucking.

"I told Oppie you'd pick him up by ten."

"Not what *time*, dumbass, *how long*. Dogs don't follow the clock. Oppie has containment phobia—you know that. It's different from escape compulsion or separation anxiety. And one other thing: stop fucking giving Oppie cheese!"

"I don't give him cheese."

"I know you give him cheese. Le Salon told me. It's the cheese from your fucking morning panini."

"Jesus! What do they do, examine his fucking shit?"

"Yes." She shot a look at her friend to screw up her courage. "James, have you been drinking?"

Shit. She was calling me James.

"I've got work to do," I said, leaving Kitty with her support-group friend.

I went into my study and woke up the PC. I had to post something on *Surge* this week for the next round of sackcloth-and-ashes protests. I rolled a joint, poured myself a scotch, and got started on my research.

A lot of what I found on the Pax Kyrie website was not all that extremist. There were announcements for planned actions in Los Alamos for the Trinity Birthday on July 16; there were melodramatic diatribes from Father Jim Darling, S.J.; and there was a page called *Evidence from Their Own Mouths* with the predictable epigram: *Those who live by the sword shall die by the sword.*

I watched a YouTube of last year's Birthday affair. It was cheap and cheesy: mic stands, speakers, hippies handing out little plastic baggies of ashes to the milling crowd. Fr. Jim Darling, their leader, speaking over the crackling PA in Ashley Park:

All right, people, at 2:45 we all drop our ashes on the ground. Then you sit wherever you are and we commence the thirty minutes of prayer. While you talk with God, Pax Kyrie invites you to ask for the miracle of nuclear disarmament. Right at 3:15, after the thirty minutes of prayer is over, we all come back and sit down on the lawn. If anyone has any questions, ask Bud here in the red hat. Now, take a deep breath. Relax. Enter into the presence of the God of Peace who asks us to be His witness. Bless us as we commemorate the horrific suffering of the victims of Hiroshima and Nagasaki. Lord, disarm our hearts as we come before You and pray, "Spare Los Alamos from your wrath that all may see the error of their ways. Let men put on sackcloth and cry mightily to God, turning from their evil ways and from the violence that is in their hands. Disarm the nuclear arsenal in Los Alamos and all the nuclear weapons on the planet." We ask this in the name of the God of Peace. Ah-men.

Nice prayer. Where had he lifted that line? I Googled *sackcloth* and *violence in their hands*. There it was in the Old Testament, Book of Jonah.

I created a new post on the *Surge* blog and typed:

The sackcloth-and-ashes people will be back this month. They model themselves after Jonah of the Old Testament, but Pax Kyrie activists should read a little closer in the good book: Nineveh was already exonerated before Jonah came along, and all his doom-mongering was irrelevant. If the leaders of the sackcloth-and-ashes protests stopped taking verses out of context to suit their demagoguery, they would realize that they are destined to end up alone, like Jonah, under the withered squash blossom: embittered, alienated, and ultimately suicidal. Modern pariahs, they only embarrass themselves. It's all right there in the OT.

Save draft. E-mail Golz for a declassify in the morning.

Kitty went up to bed without a goodnight and I started to get a headache. I lay down on the living room couch.

T he bedside clock says 6:20, and Ned is already out on his immaculate lawn. I go outside and step over the Los Alamos Monitor.

"Good morning! Did you hear a noise?"

He squints at me through the plastic goggles. Never mind. Was it just the sound of myself jerking awake?

Ned stoops to yank the cord, once, twice. The streetlamps burn on Pajarito Road, the asphalt disappears, my eyes follow the curve, and I see a cloud of smoke and ash coming around the bend.

"Ned! Look!"

He turns, reels. The storm is almost upon us.

A truck roars out of the cloud, darting back and forth on Pajarito Road—the rattling wheels, the racing engine. Through the windshield I see the driver and feel myself shudder. His clothes are on fire.

I have to warn them.

The truck crashes up on the sidewalk, barely missing me and mowing Ned right under the axle. It grinds to a stop and the driver falls out on his hands and knees, his clothes on fire. He is clawing at his face, raking at his eyes.

Tell them what you see.

I awoke with a start. My fingers and hands were numb. The nightmare had left me with a terrible feeling, as if the skin had been torn off a moment that was yet to be, a reality bound to happen.

I stayed awake drinking coffee and went into work early. Golz said, "I declassified your Pax Kyrie post and e-mailed you a new CLR."

Classified Leak Response.

It came across my desk as a veiled rebuttal in the passive voice from SAP. The Lab usually admitted to wrongdoing only when there had already been a leak.

> *Los Alamos National Laboratory acknowledged this week that several thousand drums of radioactive waste had been stored on pallets in tents just a mile upwind from White Rock, but that situation has been mitigated.*

I poked around the Pax Kyrie site some more. When I scrolled down, *Evidence from Their Own Mouths* contained a long list of safety violations at Los Alamos, and many links to documentation on the Department of Energy's own website.

I was amazed at how much of it was unclassified. Some of it was actually on Wikipedia. One memorandum detailed a contaminated-waste storage pit known as Technical Area 54, Area G.

The National Laboratory announced a plan to reinforce Technical Area 54. 20,000 drums are still temporarily buried at Area G, and thousands of additional drums are slated to arrive for above-ground storage, adding up to about 50,000 drums now or soon to be stored above ground at Los Alamos.

When I dug a little deeper, I learned that *buried* could mean that one layer of drums was under two inches of sand while the rest were stacked four pallets high beneath plastic tents.

Somewhere in the back of our minds, all Lab employees suppressed images of the drums. They were metal, fifty-five gallons, emblazoned with the radioactive warning, and there were a lot of them. Perhaps it was human nature for us to remain willfully ignorant as to the exact number.

Albeit among the biggest, Area G was just one of the Lab's 1,900 solid-waste sites in and around Los Alamos. There are hundreds of thousands of drums of radioactive and explosive waste stored under big tents all over northern New Mexico.

I had always known we were living within the perimeter of a certain amount of high explosives and radioactive waste, but I never realized just how much.

After typing up my notes from the Ogawa interview, I went into Golz's office and said, "I want to propose a story about a house."

"You mean like the house at Otowi Bridge? You did one of those last fall."

"Not a Los Alamos house. I want to do a profile on

a house over the mountains. I found it when I went camping."

Golz frowned. "What's this all about?"

"It's got a history that's kind of interesting, and it's been stuck in my mind ever since I went there. I think a little feature might be the way to get it out."

"We don't do features on houses. We do features on people. *Our* people."

At lunchtime I decided to leave work early and play a round.

I got the golf bag out of the garage and popped the trunk to load up the clubs when I heard Kitty snarl at me from the kitchen: "Where the fuck is Oppie?"

"Fuck if I know."

"I haven't seen him all day. Didn't he sleep downstairs with you last night?"

"I thought he slept in your bed."

Oops: our bed.

"James, where the fuck *were* you on Sunday?" She was calling me James again . . . and implying that if I hung around the house a little more frequently I might have seen him.

"On assignment for the magazine. Don't worry, Kitty, he's probably taking a nap somewhere. Have you checked the laundry basket?"

"I've checked fucking everywhere!" She began to cry. "I knew we should have gotten that chip implant . . ."

"That's crazy, Kitty. You're treating Oppie like a goddamn child."

"He is a goddamn child!"

"Listen, I'm going to play a round. If you haven't found him by the time I get back, we'll try the pound."

"Oh, Christ, not the pound!"

I slammed the trunk and started the car to drown out Kitty's sobs, blasting Vivaldi while backing out of the garage, telling myself, *It's hard to believe I put up with this.*

I hurtled off the Hill to the valley below, past the stone marker at the switchback, the Spider hugging the curves with a gravity that nailed me to the bucket seat, the clubs rumbling around in the trunk.

I skidded in the gravel of the Black Mesa clubhouse parking lot and jumped out of the car. It was almost one o'clock. It would be difficult to get a tee time, so many doctors taking the afternoon off.

When I popped the trunk I got hit with the stink of dog shit. Have I parked in it? A corner of my hand towel stuck out from beneath the golf bag. Something lumpy was twisted up in it. I whipped the towel away to the perfect sucker-punch: Oppie, his body rigid, smeared in his own shit, eyes bulging forth and tongue sticking out the side of his mouth like he had been strangled.

Although the smell was repulsive, I lifted Oppie out of the trunk as if I could resuscitate him. He must have jumped in when Kitty and I were bickering, the house collar, not the travel collar, around his neck. I had slammed the trunk without realizing Oppie was in there, blasted Vivaldi so I didn't hear the growling, the whining, the scratching. He'd been jolted by the collar and rolled around beneath the bag of clubs for a while, then been subjected to twenty minutes in an oven—the temperature in the trunk reaching close to 120 degrees. Probable cause of death: cardiac arrest.

The evening of the accident (*the accident*—that's what I was calling it; Kitty called it murder), Kitty moved in with Oppie's psychic, of all people, until she could sort out "whether or not to stay in Los Alamos," whether or not to stay with me.

Stupefied, I surfed cable all night, rolling joints and

watching nothing in particular but changing channels every time a dog came on the screen.

I stood in front of the medicine cabinet. Kitty had all these unused oxycodones for her wisdom teeth. Without her around, nothing was stopping me from enjoying a few of her surplus pills. You're not supposed to chew these things, I told myself. When you crush one you break its little clock, and a million invisible springs shoot out in every direction. I shook one out and munched it up, chased it with a swallow of scotch, and made a pot of coffee.

I woke up the PC and decided to kill some time by surfing the antinuke websites. Los Alamos Study Group sounds like the name of a book club, but they archive some pretty interesting leaks from actual Lab documentation.

The Lab is supposed to close TA-54, Area G, by 2015, but in the past few years it instead expanded from sixty-three acres to ninety-three acres. Who is monitoring the Lab? Answer: the Lab. Since World War II, this branch of the DOE has been the only government agency that enjoys self-regulation, despite the fact that they are sitting on the most volatility. Only the Lab, with its self-oversight and "voluntary consent" status, could get away with saying they were working on cleaning up a hazardous waste site, meanwhile piling on the radioactive and explosive material.

The Lab planned on "temporarily storing" a lot of by-products of weapons experiments in Area G over the years. What I had not known, but could see verified on the public website of the DOE, was that there already *was* a surplus of highly radioactive material in that area, over ten million cubic feet of hazardous waste, and they couldn't or wouldn't move it, and were currently building an eight-billion-dollar reinforcement as quickly as possible, shitting their pants that someone or something—an earthquake, another fire in the surrounding national forest, a terrorist—would target it.

A link from LASG led me to a study on natural and man-made disasters by the DOE's own National Nuclear Security Administration showing that a large earthquake or airplane crash could cause all that waste to explode.

I had always known we were living on top of quite a bit of nuclear waste, and I suppose I had always known it would be explosive, but I hadn't realized it would be so easy to detonate.

I Googled *Area 54, Defense Nuclear Facilities Safety Board, safety guidelines, leaks, risks*.

In the past several years the chatter had spiked. It was there for anyone to see in declassified material: the head of DOE writing to the head of the Lab in 2010 that current risk *exceeds federal guidelines*—as in, if there's an explosion or a wildfire, there's not a fucking thing Los Alamos can do about it. The vice-chairman of the Defense Nuclear Facilities Safety Board complained that the Lab had been disregarding compliance with the department's radiation safety guidelines. And everyone pointed the finger at the National Nuclear Security Administration, a division of the DOE, for abandoning the past fifteen years of safety practices that guarded against dangerous radiation leaks.

I Googled *Los Alamos, NM*, switched to map mode, satellite view, and toggled southeast, following Pajarito Road. Area G was not hard to find. It lies less than five miles down Pajarito Road. Arcing into the sky like a sports arena, over an acre of huge fabric domes. I counted twelve roofs. The four biggest tents lined up side by side, covering two football fields. Each tent could cover more than four thousand drums, up to 2.2 million gallons of radioactive waste five miles from Central Avenue, one mile upwind of Grand Canyon Drive in downtown White Rock.

As a footprint, the satellite view of Area G looked a little like Kokopelli on his knees, or a giant squirrel rooting on Pajarito Road. I zoomed in. Google Maps goes close! Jesus, how much detail was I going to get? Tents— the giant tents, floating over the big top. And traffic— I could tell the make of different cars. On satellite the tents were all there. 35°49'51" N, 106°14'22" W. *It lies just five miles from here.*

Even the *Albuquerque Journal* had headlines like: *Quake Could Cause Leak.*

The federal government's approval of continued work at a Los Alamos plutonium lab despite the risk of dangerous radiation releases in a major earthquake "undermines the principles of providing adequate protection of the public, workers, and the environment," federal nuclear safety auditors complained. The right kind of accident "could lead to fires and plutonium-contaminated smoke inside the building as glove boxes break open, and . . . safety systems designed to contain the smoke could also fail, allowing the dangerously radioactive material to escape."

The right kind of accident . . . One fire, one earthquake, one bomb—connect the dots.

I decided I'd read enough for now, so I lay down on

the couch. Too exhausted to shift away from the stabi-
lizing bar pushing into my spine, I eventually fell asleep.

M orning, the lawn, the newspaper on the sidewalk.
My neighbor Ned, the Weedwacker, the cloud of ash and smoke.

The runaway truck, the driver on fire, Ned crushed beneath the wheels.

Smoke, ash, ammonia, plutonium, uranium.

Fallout.

Awful things: more neighbors—parents and children—coming out of their houses, writhing on the ground, clawing out their eyes, their own eyes, in agony, bleeding from the nose, bleeding from the mouth, bleeding from the ears and eyes, bleeding out.

Cars storming through the streets like lightning, destroying everything in their path. The rattling wheels, the racing engines, the crashes.

The noise of the explosions, the sirens, and everywhere the screams, the moans, the grieving cries of men and women, of children and animals, gone insane with horror and pain. Make it stop! Make it stop!

Tell them what you see.

See?

Yes, see—see when the eyes are closed.

Make it stop! Make it stop!

Something like a kick to the gut made me shudder and I bolted upright from my nightmare, drool all over my chin.

I got up and stood in the dark living room. The house was quiet. My heart sank into my stomach.

I remembered Oppie and Kitty and the psychic. The thought of getting in that car—the car that had killed Oppie and further fucked things up with Kitty—was too much to take straight. I popped a couple more of Kitty's oxycodones, chasing them with the scotch. The thing I liked about Kitty's pills: they mellowed me out enough with little bounces to my perspective that made me forget the dismal setbacks of the past few days for thirty or forty seconds at a time: *Look how the sun shines off that aluminum utility pole!* And so it was I faced the day, with a swoon.

It was a gray morning on the Hill by the time I drove myself to the cremation ceremony alone.

At the corner of Third and Main I saw a sackcloth-and-asher, a cute teenager who I could tell even through the burlap had a nice figure. I thought maybe I could cheer myself up with a little token gesture of peace. She held out a sunflower while I idled at the light.

I reached out, and just as she was handing it to me through the driver's-side window, a bearded guy came up to the passenger side. "Put down thy sword!" he cried, dumping a bag of ashes all over my roof. Then he spit on my windshield, the fucking freak!

The light turned green and I peeled out, trying to move before the cloud of soot drafted in my window, but the breeze shifted and blew it right back in. Trailing ash, I smoked across the intersection.

I drove up to the Eternal Friend Pet Mausoleum and a gallery of horrified, hostile expressions. How ridiculous I must have looked with my bedraggled self in the filthy Spider! You're a horror show, Oberhelm.

When the elevator lowered the little casket into the earth, I was the only one standing on my side of the hole. The brass rail was there to keep the bereaved from jumping in after the deceased domestic. Kitty sobbed in endless Kleenex and I kept my eyes on the dirt. The few times I looked up, the ladies from her support group averted their eyes, but not before I could see the resentment burning in them for what I'd done to Oppie, what I'd done to Kitty.

There was one guy I didn't recognize in an expensive blue suit. I figured it had to be Kitty's pet psychic, Lars. Great, so this is the guy I've given Kitty an excuse to shack up with: handsome, monobrow, intense gaze.

In a crowning disgrace, my nose started bleeding. Nobody handed me a handkerchief. I ruined the sleeve of my wool suit jacket.

At the end of the service, the director handed me the bill and intoned, "Payable upon interment." I gave him my check card, and a minute later the pet mortician came back expressing condolences. "I'm afraid it was declined."

I didn't have the strength to argue with the guy and

tell him to run it again. He took all the cash I had in my wallet and said he would send me a bill for the balance.

I drove my ash-covered sports car to the lot behind the Central Avenue Grille and took myself on a one-person wake for Oppie. I guess it's a lie to say there are no bars on the Hill, but the Central Avenue Grille counts only in emergencies.

I parked on Central Avenue, and since something was wrong with my check card, I dug in the Spider's ashtray for coins and managed to come up with $4.50. I almost considered going to Smith's instead, where this chunk of change would buy me two twenty-four-ounce Cheladas, but then I would have to drink in the parking lot, and I was already having a string of bad luck.

I pushed my change across the bar, just enough for the special: a shitty light beer. This goddamned Hill!

I was staring at a boxing match on the TV for less than a minute before I heard someone down the bar order an O'Doul's. I felt him staring at my reflection in the mirrored bar back, and when I looked up it was Monobrow, the handsome guy from the funeral.

"Did you buy a Rolex this morning?"

A Rolex? No, but it felt like I just invested in a half-stake in a doggy mortuary. "What the hell are you talking about?"

"I think you might need some help," he said.

I didn't feel like getting touchy-feely with my wife's new boyfriend, even if he was Oppie's psychic. I hit my beer. "Ashley Pond is right up the road, buddy. Why don't you fuck a duck?"

My phone rang and I flipped it open.

"James Oberhelm?"

"Yes?"

"This is the fraud investigations department at Los Alamos National Bank. We noticed a spike of activity on your account. Did you purchase a designer wristwatch this morning?"

"Hold on a second." I said to the guy in the blue suit, "You're not the pet psychic?"

"The pet psychic?"

"Yes."

"No, I'm not the pet psychic." He lifted his near-beer and showed me the coaster. I recognized the design at once, but it wasn't a beer logo. It was the purple dragon of Security Awareness Protocol.

He flipped the coaster over and the dragon was gone. Now it was St. Pauli Girl with her purple bodice and big steins.

"Hang up," said the man from SAP, "I'll tell you a lot more than that bank flunky can." He came down the bar to the stool next to mine.

Under my breath I said, "You're from SAP."

"SAP is not a place. It's a process."

Conversant in SAPese, I corrected myself: "I meant to say you're part of SAP."

"We're all part of SAP."

"I know."

"What exactly do you know?"

"That there's nothing to know," I recited, "only what to forget."

He nodded. "My name is McCaffery." He didn't extend a hand. In a daze I muttered my name and he said, "I know. And the other day you shared a drink at the seediest bar in Española with a short-order cook who

I'd be surprised if you know even 10 percent of his rap sheet today."

Shit. Think quick! Shuffle through the events since you met Sunshine at Red's. There had been nothing confidential, nothing FOUO in any of the subjects or contexts, and it hadn't involved any other Lab employees. As far as McCaffery was concerned, it should be no big deal, and it had started at Red's.

"Nothing, nothing at all. I just met him at a bar and found it interesting that he called himself Sunshine, an old hippie from back in the day."

"It's in our interest to determine whether this Sunshine is a Person of Suspicion." Nice word choice. *Our* interest: did that mean *theirs* or did it mean *yours and mine*? McCaffery had me by the balls: the last thing I needed on my record was a POS.

"I'm a reporter for *Surge*, as I'm sure you know, and I thought he might tie into my journalistic research."

"Do you have clearance for this research?"

"No, but . . ." I wanted to tell him, *I don't need your fucking clearance*.

McCaffery flipped open his phone and showed me a mug shot of Sunshine, a.k.a. Harold, a.k.a. Shorn Anderson. "Your identity thief," he said. "On Sunday, when you went to pay the check at Red's in Española, he followed the waitress and said he wanted to charge it to a different card instead. By last night his associates had emptied all your accounts: checkings, savings, and money market."

Son of a bitch! Well this fucking sucked.

"Did you give him anything else? Any logins or passwords to computers at the Lab?"

"No . . . I mean, hell no!"

"Is there anyone else involved in this?"

I might have told McCaffery that I didn't know anybody else I would ever consider meeting at Red's in Española, but then I remembered he didn't yet know I had gone there specifically to meet Sunshine. The harm to my credit had been done but could be repaired. My primary concern now was to contain the damage that SAP might do to my job.

"No. Nobody. I was just stupid with my check card around a guy I barely knew, that's all."

"What about the pet psychic?"

"The pet psychic?"

"You just asked me a minute ago whether I was the pet psychic."

"Oh. He's just a jerk I've never even met. When I saw you at my dog's funeral this morning I thought you might be him."

"If you've never met him then how do you know him?"

"I think he's my wife's . . . new friend."

McCaffery cocked the eyebrow. "Anything else you want to tell me?"

I was thinking about my father. When I was a boy they had started asking me questions about him: the doctors, the cops, my mother. And I answered. I told them things he said, the hours he kept—anything they wanted to know. This was natural, of course. I was just a kid, and they were all grown-ups, and something seemed wrong with Dad, and I was sure the other grown-ups wanted to help him out. But in the end all they did was put him away, and that had stayed with me.

I was thinking about finding the pages with my name. The bad shit had intensified after I went back to the house and found my articles on the wall. I decided not to say anything more about Sunshine. What could I tell McCaffery: *My pot dealer introduced us?*

My last trip to Mel's preceded the meeting with Sunshine, and McCaffery had only mentioned Española, not Pojoaque, so I didn't say, *Sunshine works at the Roadrunner Diner*. I did not tell McCaffery that I had searched out Sunshine—or why. Instead I said, "I think I better call that bank back."

"This isn't so good for your dossier, Oberhelm. You have a privileged stump in the Los Alamos community. You have access to powerful communication lines. Your words are read by thousands of scientists and military personnel monthly. But you're exposing yourself to unclassified individuals, possible criminals, who could have contacts in foreign governments. People who could influence you."

"I write about retirees, about hobbies like fly fishing and flag collecting."

"There are many ways people can manipulate you useless you're aware of the possibilities." McCaffery finished his near-beer and pocketed the coaster in his blue suit jacket. He left me alone in the bar to finish my light beer.

I called the bank back and learned that indeed all three of my accounts—checking, savings, and money market—were overdrawn. I spoke very slowly and clearly: "That is impossible. There should be over one hundred thousand dollars in the money market."

"That's an awful lot to keep in a money market, sir,"

a banking advisor told me. Nobody was a banker any-more; everyone was a banking advisor, and no one could tell me exactly how bad the damage was.

Charges were still coming in. And because it had been a check card, not a credit card, which automatically accessed the money market for overdrafts, it was not covered by the same fraud protection.

"We're not sure of the total damage yet, sir. We're still getting wire-transfer orders from overseas."

I drove down to the valley in a daze and stopped at the Roadrunner Diner. There was a different cook but the same waitress, and she remembered me. I asked her if she had seen Sunshine.

"You mean Harold? I was about to ask you the same thing. When you drove away Sunday he left without punching out, and he hasn't shown up for work the past three days. Far as I know he quit, but if he didn't, he got fired."

This was not just about identity theft. This was about the pages on the wall, the nightmare, and what had happened to Oppie, what was happening to me. This was predatory.

I went back home to an empty house. I smoked weed, drank scotch, and popped an oxycodone. It took me minutes before I was back to slumming like a bachelor, shuffling around in my underwear and eating dinner over the sink.

The nightmare had come two nights in a row, and I did not want to let myself fall asleep.

I woke up the PC and Googled various combinations: *Earthquake, Los Alamos, Technical Area 54, Area G.*

I found one report I had never seen before: *Final Documented Safety Analysis (DSA) Technical Area. Department of Energy, National Nuclear Security Administration.*

The shitty, fax-style scan might have come off the copy machine in the physics department at the local community college. A PDF opened to 200 percent in the browser with cribbed notations in the margins—I thought it might have been from a classified conference of criticality nerds. Pen marks on tables like *Revised Accident Analysis Summary* (Unmitigated Offsite Doses**)*, where the first asterisk said, *Calculations based on "nonconservative assumptions in analysis" could put damage estimates 20 percent higher*, and the second asterisk said, *These are worst-case scenarios from an offsite dose consequence standpoint.*

Offsite, of course, meant the town of Los Alamos. The thing that got me is they already had standpoints. Somewhere within a baseball throw of my backyard there was probably a standpoint for offsite dose consequence. ODC.

One analysis put it at 1,795 rem.

One mile from ground zero, Hiroshima, doses of 150–300 rem yielded a 50 percent mortality rate. So about ten times what killed 200,000 at Hiroshima. A catastrophic fire stoked by hurricane-force winds—a firestorm—would be expected. I could use that sentence in only the passive voice.

> *Of the ten (10) scenarios screened into the accident analysis, the largest dose to the MEOI is the result of an earthquake or an aircraft crash into the waste storage domes . . . the maximum dose calculated by LANL of 1,795 rem.*

MEOI meant Maximum Exposed Offsite Individual. Brilliant—I hadn't realized that they'd already created an acronym for the victims. MEOI: that's you and me.

That *calculated by LANL* made me think about my job at the Lab. Eventually they were going to tell me to sugarcoat this word. It might take the form of Golz forwarding me an MQR with the message and asking: *See if you can make this readable.* And there it would be, five hundred words on aircraft-disaster drills. *Get ready to lie down in the middle of Trinity Avenue on Monday morning,* I told myself. *You'll look just like the sackcloth-and-ashes folks on July 16!*

> *NNSA's evaluation of the accident analyses shows that using conservative values for the MEOI parameters would lead to consequences being about 20 percent higher.*

In other words: don't say we didn't tell you that it's actually worse than we're telling you. P.S.: make that 2,154 rem.

The consequence analysis even without a potential 20 percent increase is seen to produce offsite doses to the MEOI that are significantly above the DOE Evaluation Guideline of 25 rem.

No shit, assholes. What would I rewrite this trash as? *The shit that's going to come down is going to nuke North America?* What would ten times the Hiroshima dose of radiation do to you? I Googled it. Wikipedia had an article on radiation poisoning.

At 500 rem:
Nausea, dizziness, leukopenia
Cognitive impairment
Also hemorrhage

At 800 rem:
Rapid incapacitation
Nausea, vomiting, severe diarrhea
High fever, shock

Get into the thousands and you have seizures, tremors, ataxia, death. In other words, that much radiation would pretty much cause what happened in my nightmare.

I ate a couple more oxycodones, smoked more pot, drank more coffee, watched more cable. I woke up the PC and tried to log on at work, but I could not access *Surge.* I tried three more times to be sure it wasn't a typo. Three more times I was denied. I couldn't believe it: had Golz cut off my authoring rights?

* * *

Toward dawn I could no longer resist. After a few seconds of falling I touched bottom, and I was back in hell on earth. The nightmare arrived immediately. I did not want to get kicked again—tell what I see.

Tell them what you see.

People, parents and children—my neighbors—come into the street, clawing out their own eyes.

Yea. Go on.

There are women in the street. There are children. Bleeding from the nose, the eyes, the ears . . .

The mountains quake at him, and the hills melt.

They cry, Make it stop! Make it stop! Make it stop!

The city on the Hill shall be exiled and carried away.

I woke to find the sheets wet with sweat. Kitty was not there. I was alone, but the cries echoed in the room. My neighbors were asleep in the houses up and down Pajarito Road. The bloody eyes—what were they beseeching me? I couldn't make sense of it. I was beginning to think I had to tell someone about these dreams.

When I got to the office I put my hand on the ID screen and the door did not open. I called Golz. "Sheila, what's going on?"

"It's on account of the identity theft, James. We have to reset all your clearances until we can confirm there has been no security impact. It's just temporary. Take a few days off until we can iron this out."

"Can't I come in for a minute to get some stuff?" I couldn't think of any stuff I needed to get, but before I conceded taking a day off I wanted to feel this situation out a little further.

"Don't sweat it," she said. "Just take a sick day or two."

"Is that it? Is this how it comes down?"

"I'm sorry, James."

"I can't believe this."

"I'll call you when I know something, okay?" She rang off, as they say in Europe. Don't say she hung up on me.

It took me all day Thursday to get my identity back, and by the time I did it was worthless. The money market had been a little too closely connected to the checking account. Now all of my accounts were frozen, and everyone I spoke to told me to call back next week.

I did not sleep. I smoked weed. I had already smoked half my week's weed. I knew that if I slept I would return to my nightmare. And I knew I would miss Kitty worse when I woke up.

Every time I started dropping off I shuddered in reflex before letting go. Every time I shut my eyes my nightmare hit like a punch in the gut, blowing the wind right out of me, so that the mercy of sleep was shot to hell. *Don't close your eyes!* The edge of sleep a shadow always receding, then the awful seizure—torture. *Pass along the message.* Can't I just shut my eyes for a second and give myself a break? It would feel so good to just doze off . . . *Don't!*

I went to the fridge, raided Kitty's cheese drawer, lay on the couch with a big wedge of brie and *Valley of the Witches*, and read:

> *A brujo might choose his victim deliberately for reasons of vengeance or at random to sharpen his art. Slowly, secretively break down that person's physical and psychological resistance. Poison, harassment, and hexes gradually sicken and kill a rival, a husband's mistress, or a boy in the village who was just a bit too beautiful.*

On Friday morning I went into the garage. The ash on my car had been baked by Thursday's heat and solidified by the cool of night. I remembered my financial situation and took the change jar from the laundry room. I had no idea what the day would bring, but I didn't feel like being caught off the Hill again with only Lord Calvert in the stores. My accounts were frozen and Oppie's ceremony had burned up all my remaining cash, so I went into my study and got the liter of scotch. I stuffed it under the driver's seat and put Kitty's pills and the change jar on the passenger seat.

At Starbucks I paid $12.75 with quarters and left eight cents in the tip jar. I couldn't even eat my morning panini after realizing I wouldn't have anyone to give the cheese to. A big lump rose in my throat, and when I tried to melt it with a twenty-eight-ounce Café Heeganty I almost choked. I threw my breakfast in the trash and went back to the Spider for a slug of the scotch.

I had an appointment to talk about the latest lipid tests, and I sat in the reception area at Farmer's clinic. They got me in an examination room and a few minutes later Farmer came in wearing his doctor duds. He closed the exam room door.

"James, you look awful."

"Nice to see you too."

"Mary told me about Oppie."

"I'll stop by for a drink after work and tell you the whole story. Meanwhile, can you prescribe me something that will let me get some sleep—the dreamless kind?"

"I can't give you anything. I can't even offer you a drink." Farmer slid into doctor mode and handed me the blood results. "I've got to take you off the statins immediately. Your liver is off the charts, and look at the lipids." He pointed to the LDLs. These were not the happy lipids. "Have you been taking any additional medications? Tylenol?"

"No. Unless . . ." I thought about Kitty's pills. "What is it they cut codeine with?"

"Jesus, James. Let me look at that hand."

"It hasn't been hurting."

"Not if you've been popping oxys it hasn't." He lifted the bandage from my tent-stake wound and made a not-so-bedside-mannerly face. "Look at the redness around the edges, the swelling. We're going to have to put you on a series of antibiotics."

"Hank, lately I've been thinking it's possible something might be going to happen."

"What?"

"Have you ever thought about the possibility of an emergency in Los Alamos? A really big one?"

"Sure, we're all trained for it one way or another."

"Ten times more radiation than they got at Hiroshima—what would that do to you, you think?"

"Nausea, severe leukopenia."

"What's leukopenia?"

"A decrease in light blood cells, the kind you get

with chemotherapy. There might be a sudden and severe destruction of platelets, and that might result in some bloody discharge."

"How about a hundred times more radiation?"

He frowned like someone playing a doctor on TV. "I don't know. Seizures, tremor, ataxia. Total breakdown of the nervous system."

"Could it make a sane person claw his own eyes out?"

Hank caught himself. Or Dr. Farmer caught Hank. "You're under a lot of stress, James. It's only natural for the mind to make irrational associations, especially at a time of psychological vulnerability."

"Shit, Hank, did you just say *psychological*?"

"You know what I have to recommend, and it's not just for professional liability—I'm saying this as a friend."

"Aw, hell no, Hank. Stop. I'm not listening. Just let me go."

He made me take a scrip for penicillin, but I was past the point of worrying about a little cut on my hand. I didn't tell him about the nightmares.

B ack in the Spider I checked the phone for my schedule. The week before I had made an appointment for a *Surge* interview with a scientist-gardener, and I thought it would be best for things at work if I just proceeded as normal and kept the date. Miss one month's paycheck now and everything would end up underwater: the car, the house, my life . . . Connect the dots.

I was sitting across from a kindly old scientist in thick-lens eyeglasses. I didn't have a fresh notebook, so I was taking slapdash notes on the backs of some tire store receipts I'd found in the glove compartment. I wasn't keeping control of this one. Instead of telling me about his philodendrons, the subject was talking about his prostate. But I was still supposed to be taking notes. I was always supposed to take notes.

"It wasn't the full surgery—not yet. It was more like a scrubbing to clean out the garbage disposal. You know, like a bottle brush . . ."

It was a hot summer afternoon. The cookies, Pepperidge Farm Chessmen, glistened on the plate. It was getting late. We hadn't even touched on his hobby. He wheezed to his wife, forty years younger, to set an extra place. We'd go on talking over lunch. This was against all my rules of protocol: get the story, get out, never befriend them. I caught glances of the poor wife through the kitchen door and saw an expression on her face that said embarrassment mixed with homicidal rage, like, *He's caught another one, and now I'll have to listen to the same crap all through lunch for the hundredth time while he bosses me around.*

I interrupted: "There's a house I've been going to."

The subject stopped short. "What?"

"There's a house I've been going to, over the mountains in Mora County." He looked at me quizzically. "Nobody has lived there for years. I think it's got some strange energy to it, though. Witches meet there—modern witches." The wife peered in from the kitchen. Drying her hands on her apron, she cocked her head to the side and looked at her husband. The subject's expression transformed before my eyes, and I realized he saw me for what I really was: unkempt, unshaven, a kook. Outside at the edge of his pristine lawn, the Spider, caked with ash, was parked like a car advertising a horror show. I continued, "Or teenagers with a dark obsession . . ."

The phone rang and the subject stood up. When he walked past me, he glanced over at my pad and saw what I had been doodling while he spoke: little L-shaped boxes. I heard him in the kitchen: "I see . . . No problem at all. Yes, we'll do it another time."

The subject suddenly remembered that he and his wife had other plans for lunch. He had to get ready to leave. Would I mind showing myself out? He would call the editor in the morning to set up another time for the interview . . .

Humiliated, I stumbled out of the house with my pen and scrap paper and climbed into the Spider.

My cell phone vibrated. No ID.

I figured I couldn't afford any more bad news, but I

also couldn't afford not to get good news, so I took the call. "Hello?"

There was the clunk and clatter of a desk phone coming off speaker. "Oberhelm?" It was McCaffery.

"Yes."

"Are you aware that you've been suspended from service on administrative leave?"

"Maybe. Yes, I guess. This morning my hand didn't work in the scanner."

"You shouldn't be there right now. You have to desist all work related to the Lab."

Through my mind flashed a mental list of things so far that had gotten fucked up: laptop, camera, bank accounts, credit cards, Oppie, Kitty, liver, and now job. I said to myself, *Ever since I went to that house, my whole life has been going to shit. Connect the dots.*

McCaffery said, "Meet me on Pajarito Road, your house, in fifteen minutes."

"Are you sure—"

Click. McCaffery hung up.

I reached between the seats for the pill bottle and shook out another oxycodone, chewed it. I tossed my nonsense notes on the floor and put the Parker back in my shirt pocket. That's when I felt a soreness in my chest. Was this it already, the coup de grâce? But the pain was superficial, more a burning on the surface of the skin than anything arterial. I unbuttoned my shirt and noticed a long red welt rising like a badge on the skin above my left breast. Now what? I buttoned back up and drove home to Pajarito Road. The pill kicking in, I started to loosen up.

I stood in the kitchen and it had become horrible,

a reminder of what could have been. The effect of the yellow paint on the walls was grotesque. The sunlight struck me as out of place.

McCaffery did not sit. "Why have you been Googling conspiracy theories on Area 54 and researching antisecurity freaks like LASG?"

Christ! I didn't know how closely these jerks were watching me. "Can't sleep."

"Look, Oberhelm, let's figure out what our needs are. You need some safety and stability returned to your professional file . . . Am I right?"

Don't say anything about the house in Ledoux or Ritchie Motherfucker. McCaffery didn't know about the blood tech. As far as SAP was concerned, the trouble started with Sunshine. "I want my life back," I said.

McCaffery looked at me with weary eyes. "I'm going to make my recommendation straight to you, off the record. Get out of Los Alamos. Go away for a few days."

"You think I'll be able to keep my job?"

"It's going to be harder for you to keep it in jail."

"I better . . . I better take some time . . ."

"That would be great. Take some time off. Don't let yourself obsess over this."

"I'll get a flight to L.A. The other L.A. Hollywood, L.A."

"There you go. Take in some movies. Go to the ocean. You got any money?"

"I have enough frequent flier miles." And I did.

"Can you make it this weekend?"

"Yes."

"It's going to cost you a lot of miles."

"I know."

"Just don't try coming into work again. Don't contact any Lab employees until we can sort this thing out. Okay?"

"Okay."

After McCaffery left I drank some scotch and popped a few oxycodones. I woke up the PC and checked my frequent flier balance. I found a Sunday-afternoon flight to L.A. and a cheap hotel on Venice Beach, booking the ticket and the room purely with miles, the one thing the identity thieves had not thought to cash in. It started to get dark and I made a pot of coffee.

All night I smoked and watched cable. I went through all my weed. I did not want to see the nightmare again.

I took the jar of change from the laundry room to Smith's. After the Coinstar machine took its cut, I brought my ticket to the customer service desk, and the cashier was as surprised as me to see that it had come out to forty dollars on the nose.

I headed back to Mel's and banged on his trailer door in the silence between two cumbias. He let me in and I followed him to the stove.

"Sunshine stole my fucking identity."

"Ain't that a bitch." Mel pulled on a joint and hawked something semisolid from deep down in his chest, bull's-eye against the side of his red-hot Scandia. The water in it steamed off in a few sizzling seconds and left behind a black badge of tar.

"He got a lot of money."

"*Someone* got a lot of money. That Sunshine was always too much of a weasel to do anything right on his own."

"You could have mentioned some of this."

"I never told you to go looking for him. Besides, you're the one came around asking about the Johnson house. What'd I say? When you walk up to a house like that . . ."

"Walk away."

Mel spat another tarry phlegm ball. The coating on the stove was made up of black patches of the sticky resin from Mel's throat. Thousands of badges layered the sides and top of the log burner, one for every useless night spent chugging Milwaukee's Best. I looked down at my injured hand and saw a similar coating of such crud on the bench where I sat. I choked back a gag.

I said, "He told me the whole story of Ritchie Motherfucker."

"Sunshine always was a terrible cook." Mel grinned a black smile. A pocket of trapped air exploded in the fireplace. "Did he tell you about the dreams?"

"What dreams?"

"All that week he was dying of the gangrene, Ritchie had these dreams."

"What kind of dreams?"

"Nightmares about something horrible happening on an Indian reservation. He said the name, said he had to warn them: Church Rock. I had never heard of it, but I knew it was like a natural monument, right? Ship Rock, Window Rock, Church Rock . . . I didn't put any stock in it. Figured he was raving on account of the fever, but he wouldn't shut up about it. We checked the news. Someone even found the number for the fire department in the town of Church Rock, New Mexico, and called to find out if anything bad had happened. Nothing. We told Ritchie nothing was happening, but he kept having these nightmares, awful nightmares—nobody even wanted to be around to hear him tell them when he woke up."

I felt I needed air. "Go on."

"Then right after he died we heard that name again: Church Rock. It was all over the news. A dam broke at a uranium mine and flooded the Rio Puerco. Some Navajo kids had been wading in filling buckets."

"When was this?"

"1979. But it was just a bunch of Indians in a ratty little res town, so nobody ever hears about it. It happened on the day Ritchie died, July 16."

"The Birthday," I said.

"What?"

"Nothing."

I gave Mel my forty bucks and he gave me a bag of pot. Back in the Spider, the list of names on the inside of the Mudslide carton was there on the passenger seat. I took out the Parker and crossed one out: ~~Mel Woburn~~.

Why didn't I tell somebody? Why couldn't I ask for help? I wanted to believe the nightmare wasn't real, but it was also more specific than that: I was trying to pretend I hadn't been chosen individually. Why the passive? I didn't know who or what had chosen me. Sunshine, the nightmare, the house? What was it about me that had made something choose me? Was I just unlucky? Was I fated to be prey? I was past the point I could have let it go, past where the house would let me go. Why was this happening to me?

When I got back to Los Alamos I Googled *Church Rock 1974*. On July 16 of that year, 1,100 tons of radioactive tailings in one hundred million gallons of toxic water had flooded the Rio Puerco. Kids playing, women washing clothes, men bathing—all subjected to six thousand times the allowable exposure to radiation, whatever the fuck *allowable* means. It backed up sewers, lifting manhole covers in Gallup and rolling on across the Arizona border. Today, seventy miles downstream, they can still meter radioactivity way off the counter.

Church Rock—it didn't sound like a place that had been nuked, but the testimonials that came up on the antinuke sites were chilling: *Mama said get the wash water. Why is the river so high today? Why is it so warm? Why does it stink more than usual?* It happened just like Ritchie said, thirty-four years to the day after the first man-made nuclear explosion at Trinity, July 16.

I put the PC to sleep and lay down on the couch. I didn't want to be alone in the bedroom lying awake or watching TV. When I shut my eyes, the nightmare fried my mind.

A man wakes up in the middle of the night and hears the breathing of an infant beside him. He knows he is here for a reason, even if it is just an animal reason, and this is all that matters.

Another man wakes up and feels his wife beside him, his bed beneath him, his house around them, and it is enough.

A drunk wakes up with the flash of insight of a holy man, a message of beauty and hope, and even if the message is for him and himself alone, this too is enough.

A noise wakes me. It takes a moment before the memory of all that has happened comes crashing down on me. My limbs feel heavy. My head throbs. My heart feels like it is being crushed beneath a vast weight.

And then I remember.

I wake up with nothing but the nightmare lying there beside me. I do not want to tell anyone what I have seen, but I also cannot hold it alone. It never lets up.

Make it stop! Make it stop!

There will be no end to the corpses. They will stumble upon their vile corpses.

This is not happening.

Why does this surprise you that this shall come to pass?

Why me?

A promise from God to His followers.

What promise?

You have to tell them.

But I am not one of them.
Be the instrument, for I have already killed them.

I packed a bag for L.A., the other L.A., but before I left I got on Google Maps and typed *Ledoux, Morphy Lake*. I toggled slightly north, slightly east, and located the bend in the dirt road. I switched to satellite view and pushed the zoom to an L-shaped blur that looked like the Johnson house. It had to be the Johnson house. It was the only house around.

I drove off the Hill to the valley below, and in Española an extraordinary thing happened. Depressed and irritable, about to pop another oxycodone, I looked out the window, eye drawn by the rainbow umbrella on the sign outside El Parasol, and saw Sunshine's Volkswagen van. I turned around and spotted him eating a burrito at a picnic table. Heart pounded—the thief, eating a burrito bought with my stolen money! I hadn't had my oxys yet. I pulled into the narrow lot, blocking the table where he sat. My blood was boiling. I reached under the passenger seat for the tire iron and jumped out of the car.

"You! You—asshole!" I shouted, waving the tire iron in the air. "You stole my fucking identity!" I pulled Sunshine off the bench and sat on him. He clutched the burrito desperately in one hand and I leaned into his other arm with the tire iron. Surprise had given me the advantage.

"Jesus! Don't hit me with that!"

People in front of the taco stand had stopped eating and were staring at us, but nobody got between Sunshine and the tire iron. I took out my phone. "*Number 32*," a girl called out on the speaker.

Sunshine started writhing and I pushed down on the tire iron. "Stay put, you fucking asshole!"

"You calling 911?"

"Fuck 911! You're in deeper shit than that. You picked the wrong fucking identity to steal."

"No shit! You're the son of a bitch who never told me you worked for the Lab."

I was shaking, fumbling with the numbers, and for an old hippie Sunshine was big enough. I didn't know how long I could keep the advantage. "I can call this one guy and the whole fucking FBI will cut off all roads out of Española."

"Choppers and shit?"

"Choppers and shit."

Sunshine started to tremble, rocking back and forth. "It's Ledoux, that fucking house. Your name's on that wall."

"*Number 33*," the girl called out on the speaker. "*Number 33, carne asada*," and I thought of Oppie, tongue sticking out and eyes glassed over.

"You put my name up there?"

"No. But someone did, or why would you have gone way the hell out there?" I let up on the tire iron; Sunshine saw his window. "You know you're never going to get it straight from the feds."

"Fuck." I lowered my weapon and looked at Shorn, Harold, Sunshine, holding him there in the gravel outside El Parasol, and I believed him.

A minute ago you lived life without an antagonist. Now that you know someone is after you, everything is different. You have to be on alert. It's someone's goal to bring evil to you. Right now someone is thinking about you. Life wakes up to you. Everything is charged.

What a strange place to find out I was cursed, in front of a burrito stand on a scorching July afternoon. I thought of the articles hanging on the wall in the house, and I believed Sunshine when he said he had nothing to do with it. I had driven away from the house without looking in the rearview, feeling superstitious. Now I knew it had not been enough. It did have something to do with me, this thing at the Johnson house. And worst of all, I knew I had to go back.

"*Number 34*," the girl called, "*Number 34, chicken tacos.*"

"What kind of burrito is that you're eating?"

"Chicharrón." Pork rinds fried in lard. What I wouldn't do to eat that every day if it wasn't for the lipids being so fucked up! Just hearing him say it made my mouth start to water and my fleshy heart clutch.

"You got any cash on you?"

Sunshine nodded.

I held out a hand to help him up. "Let's go to Red's."

I drove the Spider up Riverside Drive while Sunshine followed me in his van, persuaded by my threat of calling the FBI. We came in from the oven of the asphalt parking lot and sat at the bar. Red's was subterranean and cool, and the bartender descended the three steps from the drive-through window.

Apprehensive, Sunshine looked to me to order. "Two whiskey and Cokes," I said. The bartender scooped ice, poured the well whiskey, sprayed the Coke in, and we waited until he walked back up to the drive-through window.

Sunshine said, "When you told me about that girl—that piece of ass you were chasing . . ."

"Yeah?"

"That was a setup."

"How do you know?"

The air felt a little colder and the AC sounded a little louder when Sunshine answered, "She had to get you to see your name on the wall."

I thought about the blood tech and her black fingernail polish. "Mel told me about Ritchie's nightmare," I said. "I've been having one too."

"Your name is on that wall, man. That's all there is to it. You go there, you start having fucked-up nightmares, and then bad shit starts happening to you and everyone around you."

"Who put Ritchie's name on it?"

"Fuck if I know." Sunshine looked at the ceiling of the bar and continued his story. The patterns were familiar. "The fucked-up thing is that after Ritchie died, there was a good lintel above that bricked-up window and the family was growing. We figured we'd replace that window with a door. I got my crowbar and pried out the window box. I started knocking out blocks with my old sledgehammer and what I found . . . Old man Johnson buried the family bones in that wall."

"Jesus."

"When the son did what he did, it was the middle of winter, and Johnson would have to go on living there in isolation with the corpses for weeks until the melt. The thought must have driven him crazy, if he wasn't already crazy, so instead of keeping them on ice and waiting for spring to thaw the frozen ground, he built a fire outside the barn, burned the bodies one by one, and buried the bones in the east wall of the original room. Hundred years later that's where we wanted the door, so I took some of the bones out and buried them. Only thing is, they didn't stay there."

"Someone dug them up?"

Sunshine hit his drink. "I dug them up, three nights later. I started having nightmares. I was going insane. I couldn't sleep. Built the wall back, forgot about the door. The bones *wanted* to be in that wall."

We both drank.

Sunshine said, "I thought I could change my name, hide my original identity, and be safe. But that didn't help. This place follows you. It fucks with your life. I'm getting the hell out of New Mexico. Parasol was my last stop. Don't have nothing but the chunk of change I got for your card number."

"How much?"

"Two hundred bucks."

"A lousy two hundred bucks!"

"Now they're on me hard."

"Who's they?"

"I don't even know. I never get their names. Protects the both of us. I'm just a freelancer. I get the number combo, there's a beeper number, and it's done. Before the cards get shut off, the syndicate orders some expensive jewelry or some computer shit online. They get the guy for five or ten grand. I get paid when I get paid. Someone, usually a teenage kid, different every time, stops by the diner with cash. But now a guy calls me and says, *What the fuck? Was he from Los Alamos or something?* Someone *else* stole your identity right out from under them. Someone with a lot more links, a lot more private data. This is international, serious shit."

Sunshine paid and we went out to the parking lot. We both looked at the Volkswagen. I looked at Sunshine. "How far you trying to get?"

"Far as I can. You still going to call the FBI?"

"Not today."

"Solid, bro. Give me a head start."

In the parking lot outside of Red's, I stood in the blinding sun and thought of another conjunction. Put simply, at this point McCaffery had one idea of how I might get my life back, and I had another. He could spout his SAP platitudes and sleep every night like a baby. I had a different idea. I had seen what the house could do to someone's life.

I got back in the car and found the bottle under the driver's seat, chewed three more of Kitty's oxycodones, and chased them with the scotch. I glanced at the box on the passenger seat and took the Parker out of my pocket. I crossed out another name. *Sunshine*. I stared at the only one that remained: *Blood tech.*

There were some unanswered questions for the blood tech. I decided to spend one more night in New Mexico and pay a visit to the health clinic in the morning.

The pills started working. The liquor washing over them created a magic potion, and the sun through the windshield reminded me of the simple things I still had that nobody could take away from me. I could smoke some weed. I could have a drink. I stared at the bottle and counted the remaining pills: twelve. Don't let me grow to like this too much. Now is the time to smoke a joint. That joint will take this feeling and freeze it before it tips to bad, bummer, comedown, crash. Someone is hunting me, eating away at me piece by piece. A hundred miles away over the mountain range there is a house . . .

I sat at the PC. I was a dot of light burned onto an empty screen, and there were all these other dots burning around me. I could no longer distinguish myself from the static all over me. I knew that all of us together made a code, spelled a name. Connect the dots.

I closed my eyes and I saw them. I saw the blood tech and the bandage on the crook of my elbow. I saw the Johnson boy with his axe. I saw Ritchie Motherfucker and the wall of water. I saw the smoke, the rolling wall of smoke. That's the one thing that was mine. *I have to warn them.*

When I got to the community health center, the receptionist was on the phone. I asked the unsmiling records manager to check for a blood-draw order and she asked for my ID.

The records manager went back to the file cabinets and I watched her rifle efficiently through the middle drawer. When she got to the right file, she pulled it out and flipped it open. Her mouth and nose pinched like she smelled something foul and she peered over the edge of the folder at me. What note had the blood tech left? What trouble was recorded there to make the records manager look so dour?

She went into the back office of the supervisor, another beauty-marked ogre with a beehive hairdo. A conversation ensued which I could not hear, but with my nerves already edgy as hell, plus the gesticulations of the records manager and her supervisor and the frequent glances through plate glass at me, I felt like an offending bug pinned on a tray. I rubbed the painful welt on my chest.

The supervisor came out. The records manager stood beside and a little behind her boss, as if she felt she might be needed for backup.

"Mr. Oberham?"

"Yes. Oberhelm."

Both ladies grimaced. "Could I see some ID, please?"

"I just showed it to—"

"I'm going to need to see your ID." So again I pulled out my wallet. The supervisor studied name, address, birth date, and again glared at my face. "Are you sure this is you?"

"Of course it's me. Doesn't it look like me?"

The supervisor glanced around. She didn't want to say what she had to say aloud in the reception area, but she didn't want to invite me back to her office, either. She just wanted me to leave.

"Let's step over here." She took me by the elbow and got me in the eye of the automatic exit doors. Open they slid, which made it natural, however awkward our interposition, to step through the vestibule into the blinding light of the parking lot together. "I'm afraid I can't help you."

"Why not?"

"These health records have been sealed."

"But they're my files. I can sign."

"Even if you are who you say you are, there's a lien on this file. These records have been sealed by the county medical examiner."

"I don't understand." As I said it, her words rang in my mind: *medical examiner*. It's the euphemism for coroner. "They're saying I'm dead?"

"Your file has been closed."

"This is preposterous—I'm standing right here!"

"You have to clear this up with the county. I can't do anything for you now."

I stood in the clinic parking lot. Nobody could help me. I had nowhere to go.

Driving. Driving was the way to stay awake. I got

in the Spider and turned left onto 68. I stopped at Blue Heron Brewery and asked the ale wife for a sample.

Back in the Spider my cell vibrated. Caller ID said *OGAWA H.* Just seeing his name there was like a greeting from a time not too long ago, before everything had started going to shit, so I answered.

"Hello, Harumi-san."

"James Oberhelm?"

"Yes."

"Thank god! You still have that pen I gave you?"

"Yes. I'm sorry, I forgot to thank you. It's a very nice—"

"Would you please come to my house immediately and bring it with you?"

I drove back through the valley and up the Hill. When I got to Ogawa's house, he was in the doorway leaning on a walker, his wife also supporting him. "You have it?"

"Yes."

"Thank god!" He slowly struggled to his chair in the living room and I followed. I sat across from him in the same chair I had used before. After Ogawa was settled, his wife sat down on a sofa that faced the space between us. The great chief criticality officer said, "I don't know how I could have let this happen. I unintentionally gave you something of great personal value that also may be hazardous to you."

"The pen?"

"It is an atomic pen. We made a handful of prototypes in the 1960s for the Parker Company. There is a brief scene in *2001: A Space Odyssey* where one of the astronauts floats with the pen in a weightless chamber.

As I was a consultant on the film, Mr. Kubrick made me a gift of one of the prototypes. When I told my wife to bring a boxed gift from the shelf in my library, I never considered that she may have picked up the pen, which I had taken out to look at that morning."

He glanced at his wife and for the first time I could see that she had been crying.

"I left it on my desk instead of replacing it in the safe. Only now did I discover it missing. In a metal safe it does no harm . . ." He frowned, staring at my shirt.

I looked down and there it was in my breast pocket, right over where the welt was rising. I pulled it out, walked over to him, and handed him the pen.

He put it gently down on the table. "Please, sit down," he said.

"I'm afraid . . . my clothes are not very clean."

"No formalities, please. Have a seat."

I sat.

"I am terribly sorry that this happened. I cannot explain it. You of course have excellent medical care through the Lab, but I would personally like to urge you to see a specialist. With your permission, I will call to make the appointment . . ."

At that moment, with Ogawa and his wife in their living room, behind walls thickly insulated and a floor plush-carpeted by a luxurious retirement, I felt so far away from the chaos of Los Alamos—a Los Alamos that Ogawa had helped build, that his team had stewarded through some of its most tumultuous passages, and that nevertheless continued to thrive, however tenuously, as a bucolic bedroom community built on back of the Bomb—that I realized I needed to turn to him for something I wasn't sure I could get anywhere else: not from my boss, not from my doctor, not from McCaffery, and certainly not from Sunshine or the blood tech. "Harumi-san, may I speak freely?"

"Of course."

"When the incidents occurred with the Demon Core . . ."

Ogawa winced to have this brought up so abruptly, haphazardly, although of course, in the acuity of the former chief criticality officer of Los Alamos National Laboratories, the possibility of a connection to what had happened with the pen would be anything but random.

I continued: "Before either one of the events, did you ever have a sense of foreseeing the tragedy?"

Ogawa's wife turned her chin to look at him sharply, giving me my answer. I knew I had hit upon an essential question—one which the subject had long wondered if it would ever be asked. The question he had feared every day for six decades might eventually arise, but he had also come to understand after a time that most interlocutors would be too polite to consider voicing it aloud, and so it could be that in half a century he had become complacent about the question, resigned to living with the answer a secret between his wife and himself. Probably not even their children suspected there was a secret, and now, in good health for their station but nevertheless advanced in years, the Ogawas could perhaps look calmly at the horizon and know that it was going to die with them. Until I asked it.

"You mean as in dreams?"

"Yes . . . or nightmares."

Mrs. Ogawa put her head in her hands and began

weeping softly. Ogawa said something to her gently in Japanese, and she stood up without looking at either of us and withdrew into the kitchen.

"Naturally, I experienced traumatic stress and great sleep difficulty after the accidents, but there is something that Sumi and I have not spoken about, and that has been troubling to us for some time . . . Before the first incident, I dreamed of Daghlian having an accident. I told Sumi about it over breakfast, and she agreed that because Daghlian had a reputation for sloppy work, it was normal that I, the criticality officer, should bear the burden of conscience and be concerned. I made a note to schedule additional safety training for Daghlian and some of the others in our division, but I did not remember the dream again until after the accident—which, as you know, took place while Daghlian was working alone with the core.

"When the circumstances were reconstructed, the accuracy of my dream was what I found most disturbing. It was all there: the beryllium in Daghlian's hand, the brick dropping with a hideous flash onto the plutonium core . . ."

"If you will allow me just one further query, Harumi-san. It has to do with a matter of great importance to me, although I fear there is nobody else I can speak to about it . . ."

"Go on."

"If you could go back to that morning in 1945—"

"Yes," Ogawa interrupted.

"Yes?"

"Yes, I would tell Daghlian about the dream."

"Even though you might bring upon yourself some . . . ridicule?"

He fixed my gaze with the intensity of the confident physicist who had overcome a thousand obstacles—not least the unapologetic suspicion of even his closest colleagues for being Japanese—to earn one of the top classified positions in the military-scientific complex during the headiest war in modern history. Ogawa leaned forward and I saw a flash of temerity in his eyes. "It has been more than sixty years, and not a day has gone by that I wished I hadn't chosen to live with the shame of public disgrace over the guilt of my silence."

I assured Ogawa I would go right to the hospital for an evaluation and that I would call him as soon as I had news. We were both a little stunned. The esteemed officer of risk abatement gave me a strange look as if to say, *Criticality is high around you.* He let me leave with these words: "The scorn of others, even their utmost contempt, softens with each day. But the edge of remorse cuts sharper with every waking."

In strict observation of custom, he gave me another gift to replace the one he had requested be returned. Salad tongs.

I left Ogawa's house feeling strangely elated. Certainly the oxycodones were contributing something, but a simple judgment of "drug-induced" cannot overshadow what I experienced as a delicate combination of complex perceptions: exhaustion, terror, hope, duty. I was past thinking I had to tell someone about these dreams. I was thinking I had to tell *everyone* about these dreams.

What if it turns out to be a false alarm? It doesn't matter, just so long as you get this nightmare off your back. Spread the nightmare, distribute the burden of seeing what you see, knowing what you know. If it's just a delusion it won't hurt anyone else, and what else have you got to lose?

And if it really is a sign . . . then there is no time to waste, and you have to send the message. There is someone with a gun to your head, and that someone is you, and the gun is inside your head.

I stopped by Pajarito Road. Gently I massaged the welt on my chest and woke up the PC. My eyes were weary, so I dimmed the screen before typing. I opened a blank Word document and started writing down the list of things that had gone wrong—*laptop, camera, wife, dog, money* . . . Under *job* I typed: *life*.

What good does it do me, knowing what I know, seeing what I've seen? What had it taken, a little over a week? Just like Ritchie Motherfucker and his gangrene, his visions.

As I typed I felt myself letting go. Things had spun so far out of control that there must be a story to work through. Maybe I would come out ahead on the other side. Something that could salvage this experience: I could write about the nightmare. Maybe a scientist would read it and see some kind of clue, something that would mitigate risk on the Hill and save lives down the line. Things were going badly, but in a nice, simple way I was ready to do anything. I was ready to do what had to be done.

I chewed three or four more oxycodones and drank off the liter of scotch. I typed: *who? who is responsible for this?*

Not Mel Woburn. Not Sunshine. Possibly the blood tech. Each could be said to have urged me along, but did I believe any one of them was actually responsible? I had some questions for the blood tech, though the house was a different story. Maybe whether or not I believed in the house, the house believed in me. I thought about the articles hanging on the wall. I typed: *Johnson. Old man Johnson.*

My job is telling a story, just a little different from the story others tell. What if sanity is the same thing: a story that is a little different? Should the sane man gloat over it? And what if crazy is right some of the time, like Ritchie Motherfucker on the way to Church Rock?

Again I thought about *Surge*. Had the Lab really shut off *all* the passwords? Five years ago, when I started at *Surge*, I had set up the site as administrator. That had been a separate login than my contributor account. It was possible the administrator login still functioned.

I had been new at the job and there was a strange image in my head: a long roll of quilted toilet paper to pamper the asses of the Frankensteins of war. Username: *charmin.* The password had to have both numbers and capitals, and the first thing that had come to mind was some graffiti I admired down the Hill in Española. Password: *Sk8rDie!*

Up came the full-access screen for *Surge*. So that was it. I was in the system, and I reactivated my regular username, and next thing I knew I was back in as *JamesO* and prompted to create a new password.

I started typing.

A great wall of ash and smoke rolling up Pajarito Road from Technical Area 54, Area G. A storm of radiation. Just another MEOI.

A light changed. Did that come from outside or in? I don't know what I typed. I heard things. I heard things I didn't type, and I heard things I did type. I wasn't sure I actually typed the bit that caused all the trouble.

Be the instrument, for I have already killed them. Abandon the community that has forsaken you. Abandon them to ashes.

I felt the physical manifestation of despair in my bones and in my viscera. Joy is no less pathetic than the worst grief.

I let myself type. Do not sleep until it's through. Make the nightmare go away. You won't have to look at it every time you close your eyes. You won't have to hear their cries echo in the room when you open them.

I don't remember all I typed, but when I was done I hit *Save*, not *Send*. I made it to the bathroom and flicked on the light. I heard the little voice go, *Poor Dad*. I draped my arm over the toilet, my head in the bowl. Heave . . . Heave . . . Heave.

I get in the Spider and drive. The skies are dark over the Sangre de Cristo. Heavy clouds are rolling in from the west, moving in with me.

Who put my name on the wall? What does it matter who, now? The problem isn't the hunter. The problem is the trap. There is something about the house that makes me go to the dark. I keep going back. I blame myself. Nobody is doing this to me. Nobody but my own ghosts.

I drive into Mora and stop at the Mustang.

I scavenge $1.79 from the cracks of the seats and find myself a mini of the cheapest stuff: schnapps. It rings up $1.99, and I pick the last two dimes from a dish next to the register with a hand-lettered sign that reads: *If you need a penny, take it. If you need more, get a job.*

I say thanks and the Mustang attendant says nothing. I can tell from her expression that I must look like a madman.

I get back in the car and catch the weather forecast on the radio:

A weak upper-level disturbance will slide east across New Mexico today bringing rain showers along and west of the central mountain chain. Only light precipitation is expected with this first system above 7,500 feet. A more powerful storm system will move in quickly behind the first system with drenching rains at high elevations.

I look up and see charcoal sheets of rain on the Sangre de Cristo.

I pull off into an arroyo behind a willow tree on Aplanado, breaking the branch of an evergreen to conceal the chrome bumper from the road.

I have ceased to be concerned about trespassing. I come to the house this time like a natural son.

I step onto the portal. Again I feel the pressure drop, even in the cold, clammy air, even as I swoon from the pain in my chest, from the headache of insomnia, from the burden of a world collapsing on my shoulders. It is like the house draws you in to make you sleepy so that it may whisper its story in your ear.

I look at the walls. There are drugs in those walls. It's the east wall where my articles are hanging, the wall that contains the remains, the one that stands in the shadows.

I walk inside and the birds start peeping.

You still here? Your mother is stuck somewhere away from home, or else really dead. Maybe she's been dead since the day I first came back.

The padlocked hinge I pried off is still there on the floor. I stand before the wall with my articles tacked all over it, the pages fluttering.

There are bones in these walls.

The air smells beautifully of rain. How the hell did it get so cold all of a sudden?

It is time to get started. It will not be difficult to take the pages off the wall. Only Scotch tape sticks them to the hard plaster. I could tear them down in a fury, or hold a lighter beneath the bottom row of sheets and set the wallpaper ablaze.

I remove them one by one, remembering every subject through each headline, my name at the top of every page.

When I am done I have a neat pile of pages from *Surge* to take with me. *Now it's over. You can drive away. Catch that plane.*

I stand back and look at the wall. I look at the dingy paint.

This is crazy. You've taken the pages down. You can drive away, stop this stupidity, break the chain.

I get the tire iron from the trunk and dig a little at a cracked spot in the plaster.

The rain comes on quickly, tricking me into thinking it might be a brief shower.

It is too early for the monsoon-type rains of midsummer in these mountains. I have no change of clothes, the heater in the Spider doesn't work, and it is cold, so I decide to wait it out.

I keep digging.

Before I've chipped very far, I put down the tire iron to step out on the portal. The shower has become a steady downpour. I will have to wait for it to clear.

I pace around to keep myself warm. Soon the rain is coming down so hard that I know I will get soaked just stepping onto the portal. It is pounding on the roof, loud, annoying like a dinner guest who gets suddenly, rudely drunk.

It is getting on night.

I decide to leave. I will run to the car. I will get wet. I will start the car and shiver all the way back down that road. I can be down to the Mustang in twenty minutes, and there is still some loose change in the car. A hot chocolate with Lord Calvert will stop my teeth chattering. Maybe there will be a cheap, dry T-shirt: *Mora, NM. Leave here and never come back.*

I make a break for it.

I splash up the drive, jumping clumsily between potholes filled with water, getting soaked within seconds. When I arrive at the car the arroyo is running. The water in the ditch has come up above the tires.

I open the door and the floor of the car is choked with mud.

I try starting it even though I know it is stupid—not a cough, not even a click. I splash back to the house, remembering something from the Discovery Channel: once you get wet, you've lost half the battle. My shirt is cotton. What do they call it? The death fabric. The rain keeps pounding.

I stand shivering under the portal and look back at the valley, but there is nothing to see, no lights on the other side. Everything is in cloud.

You will have to spend the night in the house.

The wind blows the rain slantingly onto the portal. I turn and go back inside. The birds will not let up squeaking now, loudly, incessantly, as if some understanding in their miniscule brains makes them declare full alert. I wish there were some way I could tell them: *It's okay, your mother will be back soon.* I think about their mother. *Hell, when this rain lets up, I'll bring you some food.*

I decide to build a fire in the middle of the floor. The absentee owner will be angry when he next comes around and discovers the damage. I don't care. I have my lighter. There is dry wood inside. Wet, cold, stranded, I have to burn it. I am taking heroic measures.

I gather what scrap wood I can find from around the floors: an old chair leg, splintered floorboards, planking I cracked off the padlocked door with my tire iron. I don't have very good ventilation. A little smoke never killed anybody, I tell myself. Yes, it does—so does a little lead paint.

The pages of *Surge* are too glossy and won't get the wood going. There is only the Bible for kindling. I take my lighter out of the Altoids tin and light the onionskin pages.

I mumble a lapsed-Catholic apology in my head. It's only the heat I'm after.

I tear out a good chunk of pages and stoke the flames. A black arc sweeps across the stack, shrinking and leaving behind a pile of ash.

I start to feel better when the fire burns up a little, but I have to be right near the flame to feel warm. I am still wet, and the second I back off from the fire I get cold.

I take off my clothes, spreading them out on the planks to try to dry them.

I stand exposed in the firelight, shivering in damp underwear. I want a blanket. A sleeping bag would be better, something to wrap around myself.

I pace the floors. I have to keep moving.

Where is my marijuana? I might have thrown it in the fire. It happens all the time, people burn something of value to them by mistake.

I am growing tired. It rains.

Now it is full-on night. I pass between the bird nest and the fire. The baby birds peep weakly. A mother won't return to her nest when a person has messed with it. It's I who am keeping her away.

I fill a bottle cap with some water and hold it to the mouth of the nest. Do I feel them pecking at it? I can't tell. My hands are shaking.

Keep moving.

The chair legs burn to cinders. I use the tire iron to break up the crude table that held the Bible. I have to add paper to keep the fire going, so I throw in the glossy *Surge* articles.

I am getting better at managing this fire. How long has it been pouring? Four hours? Even if it is the monsoons, no one storm could last much longer. A warm, dry front always pushes through a cold storm system.

I collect all the trash I can find on the floor and burn that. I cast around for more wood. I take the tire iron and pry up the floorboards at the edge of the room. I burn them.

There is no noise coming from the mud nest hanging from the viga. Nothing. I should have helped them while I could still do something. Is it my fault their mother hasn't come back? I'll get them some food as soon as this rain lets up, go out in the mud and dig up some worms.

I find a rusty soup can and let water stream straight into it from the holes in the roof.

I have to piss, but I don't bother getting up and going onto the portal. I go in the corner.

I see something burning at the edge of the fire. It might be my marijuana. Or it could be the business cards from my wallet. It is impossible to tell, but I keep on looking at it in fascination. A neat trapezoid of ash has folded upon itself like an ancient and decaying silk shirt: a sleeve, a cuff, a collar. It is beautiful, and it soothes me to see it.

I feel damp, but not cold.

The cloudy sky starts to lighten a little but still the rain is not letting up. I go back into the other room and keep chipping at the wall.

I am tired. I go back into the main room and crawl onto the mattress to lie down. The springs groan, comforting my aching spine. I do not mind the foul odor.

I swoon with fatigue and listen for the sound of the rain, convinced that it has stopped and what I heard in my ears was just a ringing in the head of a man gone mad. Then I feel the floor lurch a quarter-turn, the room spin into place, and the sound come on louder than before: rain, more rain, on the roof, in the corners, puddles, pools outside, filling higher, deeper.

Trying to remember: why did I come here? Don't I have a job, a house, a wife? I just need to leave. Walk away. All I have to do is get up and walk away.

You tried that. You tried that last time you left. But your name was on the wall, so you came back.

When I go into the other rooms to pry up more splintered chunks of wood, my teeth begin chattering. I would be relieved if someone showed up and caught me trespassing, rescued me, arrested me, called an ambulance—ended the ordeal—but this wish is just a diversion from the real problem: I have to keep coming back here.

Execrate. My life has been execrated, dead on paper, dead credit, medically dead. All dead. Abandon them to ashes.

Streams of water from the ceiling are leaking all over the room and the fire has died down. My teeth are chattering uncontrollably. That's a sign of hypothermia. So I run out into the rain in my underwear and slog through the mud to the car. I dig in the glove compartment for something to use for kindling and find the Los Alamos telephone directory. Back inside the house I light my lighter and tear out the yellow pages to make a torch. While they briefly blaze, I search around the room and find some trash to burn. I sit on the mattress close to the fire.

I don't want to let sleep come again, but I am desperately tired. The storm clouds are low and it is a dark day, but I am unclear whether it is dawn or dusk.

Still raining. No dogs barking, no coyotes. Everything is in its den.

Something on the floor catches a glimmer of firelight: a rusted paperclip. I unbend it and hold the tip over the fire, heating it until the sliver of steel is orange. I touch it to my skin, to the back of my left hand and wrist, shooting pain through myself to stay awake.

My adrenaline begins to dry up and I torture myself at the edge of consciousness. I spit on a piece of wood at the rim of the fire. The water burns off leaving an archipelago of mucus in the shape of a backward J. The moldy stuffing warms me, rocks me to sleep.

I see a town of ten thousand people reduced to ashes. I see people coming out of their homes in agony. Smoke blots out the sun, fills the sky. A noise beating down on the earth makes the dying clasp hands desperately over their heads. *How horrible to foresee death so clearly.*

S omeone does come, a man in a Western hat and a long oil coat that reaches to his cowboy boots, the rain dripping from his brim and cascading off his back. I cower like a wet animal while he shines a flashlight around the room to take in the squalor.

What must this look like? My pathetic fire smolders amidst the splintered boards. My clothes in the corner make a wet, filthy knot. I am worse than the sackcloth-and-ashes people. At least they don't move into your living room in their filthy rags and use your furniture for kindling.

The man says, "I seen your car stuck in the mud, figured you could use some help."

This strikes me, after many hours of animalistic toil, as so human, so sympathetic, that I convulse into a great sob.

There are neighbors and people around who call this valley home, and I came here to this abandoned house and turned it into a demon obsession.

I have made my mark on this forsaken place, but I know that I have been bitterly defeated. It all seems preposterous, now that help has arrived. The pages with my name are ashes, but the superficial scars I have left behind are nothing to the house, just scratches in the plaster. The bite it has taken out of me will fester for a long time, maybe kill me.

There is no blanket to put over my shoulders, and

the man's coat is dripping wet. He waits while I let it out. When finally I have calmed down to the point I can breathe, I say, "It's a mistake."

The stranger nods. "You wouldn't be the first."

He walks past the fire and I briefly glimpse his face: it is the red, deeply lined face of a tough old man culti-vating a relaxed rage. He bends over me and takes out a pack of cigarettes, a brand I buy now and then when I can't sleep. I nod and the stranger fishes out two, lights them both, and hands one down to me.

I shiver on the floor in my underwear. The cigarette tastes terrible but the heat and smoke in my lungs are soothing.

The stranger does not speak of the broken boards or the scorched floor as it is clear that a greater depravity than mere vandalism led to these.

He says, "You been working on that wall?"

He walks to the splintered door and shines his flash-light into the next room at the place where the tire iron juts out between bricks.

He turns back and fishes in the breast pocket of his overcoat for a bottle of pills. "Want some?"

"What is it?"

"Sedatives. Take some."

"No thank you."

"They're very good drugs. The sort you like."

"What?"

"Everybody likes these."

"No. Not from you."

He shrugs, gazes at me strangely. There was already some in the cigarette. I am almost down to the butt by the time I notice the taste.

"You put my name here?"

He turns and looks at the wall. "Not I. The chain of names began long before this, and today you stand at the head of them all."

He goes to the viga where the nest is suspended, reaches up, and squeezes his fingertips through the hole in the nest, taking one of the baby birds in his hand. I hear a weak chirp. This one is barely alive. He turns and dangles it down before me. "You let them die."

"What?"

"The swallows. You let them die."

His face contorts into a hard, red mask. The wrinkles on his forehead settle sideways.

I don't know what to say. "They were already dead."

"Who are you that these birds should die for?"

The man drops the chick on the floor. With a prescient revulsion I turn away. When I hear the small bones crush under his heavy boot, I bow my head and vomit.

I search the floor. For what? The tire iron? It is lodged in the wall, and it will do me no good against this one.

"Don't touch that wall no more, you peckerwood bastard."

A boot to my stomach knocks the wind out of me and leaves me gasping for air, wishing I could vomit again so that the convulsions might relieve the sharp pain in my voided abdomen.

I don't speak, but the old man seems to know what I am thinking through the pain.

"Yea, I built this wall with my own hands, eight hundred bricks, each brick thirty pounds—twelve tons of earth, and more of mud between."

"I do not believe any of this. I do not believe that you are even here."

"That is a great error," he whispers close to my ear, "for we are both really here."

He goes to the wall and yanks out the tire iron, marching back across the room with it raised like a club. I cover my head in my arms.

"What animates a man like you? Women flicker onto the screen like little pictures. You smoke your drug and drink your bottle."

"You were there."

A foul grin tells me he knows I am beginning to understand. "Ye did not come easily to the realization. You had to warn the people."

"Why me?"

His smile is small and ugly. "Nahum does not go to Nineveh."

He takes off the overcoat—wearing nothing underneath. It is not easy to look at, his ass a great sagging heap that flaps around his hips. Don't try to describe the thing that's shriveled in a nest of gray pubic hair between his pockmarked thighs.

"What is it you are going to do?"

"*Naked I came out of my mother's womb, and naked shall I return . . .*"

Curled in a ball, shivering. A splitting headache. Vomit all over my shirt. Stomach throbbing from all the heaving.

Waking up to two men in hazmat suits standing over me. One of them breathes my name: "James Oberhelm?" I nod in my own vomit. PVC gloves grip my upper arms and I am sliding out of the house.

The spacemen get me outside on a stretcher and I am loaded into an ambulance and covered with a reflective blanket.

I come to slowly, the aching all over gradually worsening. I wish I could either die or go back to sleep, but the paramedics inject me with something meant to keep me conscious.

I am held at the Los Alamos Medical Center pending blood-test analysis. They put me on intravenous antibiotics for the hand, which they tell me has become infected. They inject chemicals intended to counteract other chemicals they say I have ingested, deliberately or not.

We meet in an interview room that smells like piss, the SAP agents and I.

Look into their eyes: that infuriating, patronizing vacancy. They think you're a drug addict. Make them understand your work. You're an interviewer, one of the best in the in-house publishing industry. You came to the Lab for the money, the bennies, the Cadillac health care.

There is so much you do not tell them. You do not tell them about Mel Woburn or Ritchie Motherfucker. You do not tell them about how when the hippies went to cremate Ritchie, they found out it wasn't so easy to burn a body.

You do not tell them about the wall. You do not tell them about the rain, the birds, or Fourth of July. You do not tell them about the bones or the photo. Do not tell them about the blood tech. Why not? *Because you've got to get to her first.*

"You put it on *Surge*. You posted it on the feed."

They have me there. I posted. Or someone with the administrator's password posted. It was only up briefly, but it was early in the morning on Tuesday, July 16, the Trinity Birthday.

All the scientists were home drinking coffee, reading e-mails and articles for pleasure, when a message got posted to *Surge*. It looked a little like haiku.

TA-54—
B49 CSU
LLSW
RLW
Pu-239

drum seepage
critical mass
earthquake
seismic: 7/16 18:06:06
mag: 7.1

Someone posted:

local fallout: 919 rem (+/-100)
burning eyes
burning lungs
radiation poisoning
mortality: 100 percent
avg. life expectancy: 12 hours

B49 CSU is the name of a container storage unit, larger than your average industrial storage container. It could hold more than fifty large oil drums in a single layer on pallets. LLSW is low-level solid waste, RLW is radioactive liquid waste, and Pu-239 is plutonium. Anyone in Los Alamos with an elementary education can tell you what 919 rem means. Plus or minus a hundred . . . In case anyone didn't understand, the post included mortality and average life expectancy.

That was the message. It read just like an emergency bulletin, something someone would send out when they got some very bad news through official channels that they only had time to copy-paste. It read like a collateral-damage assessment on a classified military broadcast: cold, precise, appalling. It read like something a scientist would type.

Panic ensued. As luck would have it, in an unrelated accident, before dawn a delivery truck skidded and jackknifed on its way up the Hill, closing down the road to traffic for six hours while a tow team maneuvered it out of the way. The driver got a citation for two hundred dollars; he should have taken the White Rock Road.

Most Tuesday mornings, this would have proved a nuisance to a few hundred Los Alamos residents going down to the valley to shop. Anyone important trying to drive anyplace important, like to a meeting with the governor in Santa Fe or to the airport in Albuquerque, would have just turned around and taken the back road out of town.

But people were looking at the alarming posting on their phones, they were texting and retweeting each other the message, they were calling each other and saying, *There's an evacuation notice, but the road is closed, and now they're saying it might be a terrorist attack*, and it all went viral.

The traffic was snarled all the way back through town. If you were trying to get to the medical center, you came up against mobs who had taken the gridlock-frustration into their own hands: using both lanes of narrow streets to point their cars toward the valley even though nothing was moving.

Even the Pax Kyrie protesters who were coming up in cars and church buses from the valley had to turn around and postpone a planned action. They got stuck behind the delivery truck.

And nothing happened.

No explosion. No earthquake. Not the slightest tremor on the Richter scale.

SAP, the DOE, and Homeland Security call me a national security risk. The agents' arrest report describes me as *filthy and having a foul odor*; it says I was *raving* and had to be restrained. I remain in custody, under medical observation, and on administrative leave from the Lab.

The *Los Alamos Monitor* calls me *The Surge Tweet-ker* and the *Journal* and *New Mexican* blow the dust off journalistic chestnuts like *Chicken Little* and *Benedict Arnold*. I ask the SAP investigators how they found the house.

"Unidentified caller. Can you tell us why the pages of the Los Alamos telephone directory were stuck to the wall with human excrement?"

"My excement?"

They glare.

"Can I ask to speak to McCaffery?"

"Well, you can ask . . ." Interrogation dissimulation: they say there is no McCaffery.

I tell the SAPers to talk to the bartender at Central Avenue Grille. He tells them he remembers me, "the ashes guy"—he had to wipe down the barstool after I left—but he testifies that nobody else was drinking at the bar so early that morning and that I had been muttering to myself "like some kind of meth head."

I tell them check my cell phone. They analyze the SIM card and determine that I did get a call on July 12, the day after I was placed on administrative leave, with no caller ID, but they trace it back to a banking advisor in Los Alamos. She had been trying to update me on the fraud investigation when, according to her testimony, "He babbled something about his hand, how it didn't work in the scanner," and then I hung up.

Golz announces her resignation. My life savings has been pillaged and I get no paycheck. I have no money for a lawyer, but on Thursday the eighteenth I learn that the ACLU has made me a cause and retained a defense attorney. The Jewish-sounding "Katz" inspires confidence.

We meet in the same interview room as the men from SAP. "Don't ever talk to those assholes without me in the room." I want to tell him how good I have been. I did not tell them about Mel Woburn. I did not tell them about the blood tech. He hands me a business card: *Cahats*.

Things are always not what they seem.

I tell him the truth: I was drinking, I was despondent, I have no memory of posting that message on *Surge*, but whoever did made it impossible to prove it wasn't me. *You never know how people can manipulate you . . .* I do not tell Cahats either about Mel Woburn or the blood tech.

For the moment I am suspect, soon I will be defendant, and then I will be convict.

I have no money for the bond. At the arraignment on Friday the nineteenth Cahats makes a case to get me out until the trial on the basis of a few technicalities: I am a U.S. citizen, I did not hurt anyone, and the toxicology tests conducted at my arrest determine that I cultivated a brief but serious addiction to painkillers. Cahats cites expert pharmacological testimony that oxycodone, with the right megadosing (ten or twelve pills in a twenty-four-hour period), especially when mixed with alcohol, can create dependency literally overnight.

I am released and placed on nightly house arrest and daily, court-mandated detox rehabilitation. Cahats loans me some money for groceries and counsels me to take however long I need to recover from "that bump on the head." The bump. In front of the judge he called it "schizophrenia resultant from accidental poisoning."

My first night out I watch a lot of cable. I flip through the infomercials, workouts, and reruns: everything looks the same. I forget how long I've been flipping the way you forget the last stretch of drive late at night on the highway. The only things that can make me forget the shit my life has become for a few seconds at a time are comedies from the '50s and '60s turned up as loud as the TV will blare: *I Love Lucy, Leave It to Beaver, My Three Sons*. I don't hear what they're saying, but the black-and-white relieves my eyes and the laugh tracks are a kind of white noise for my consciousness.

My cell phone has been confiscated as part of the investigation, and for me there will be no more computers for a while. The laptop was fried. The PC has been seized for a complete hard-drive search, the kind where they can recover even deleted data. They impound the Spider. Evidence. I am left alone on Pajarito Road to knock around the house in the night, and I know how bereft I am.

All the little things she did to keep me presentable.

What did Kitty used to do? Iron, button, fold? All I can do each morning is make it to the dryer to get the day's clothes.

I lie awake cycling through all that went wrong. This was your fault. This wasn't your fault. It makes no difference. This is all your fault.

I sit in the living room and turn on the TV, find an infomercial. My eyes stray to the dining room. The slider. The curtain covers all but a sliver of glass. I get up and pull it all the way to the edge. Is the latch closed? The latch is closed.

I lie down on the king-size, springless, formaldehyde-free bed. There are no more nightmares. Now what is worse is when I awaken.

I could have a drink. A drink would make me feel better. It might not be as easy as just going to the cabinet in my study—they took away the bottles when they took the computers and the phone—but I could still walk down to Smith's, pick empty bottles and cans out of trash barrels on the way, redeem them for a nickel apiece. How many would it take for the price of a twenty-four-ounce PBR? How many would it take for a forty-ounce malt liquor?

I could stand in front of Smith's and spot one of my old coworkers or a former subject and ask for a buck. Make up some excuse: locked my wallet in the car, lost my keys, left the cell at the house, need to make a call on a pay phone. Are there any more pay phones?

I could, but I don't. Something inside me knows the liquor would just magnify my misery. The only reprieve I get is in the second or two after waking. When I was doing okay, I had awful nightmares. Now there is no more nightmare. When I awaken, it takes a second or two to recover the misery. Then I feel the welt on my chest or the sore hand, and I realize that Kitty is not beside me. There is another reason I don't have a drink: because maybe if I don't, Kitty will come back.

Remember when this house was new, sitting with Kitty on the living room couch, watching *Lost* on Tuesday nights and cuddling over a big bowl of popcorn? Remember how she used to sprinkle on nutritional yeast, how our fingers would mingle in the middle of the bowl? Remember how her touch would make me tingle, how the hairs on my knuckles would stand on end? Remember how she used to stroke my arm? Remember how I used to feel it, really feel it?

Remember?

Maybe she will see how hard I'm trying. Maybe, however bereft I look, she will smell that I am clean. Maybe she will decide to stay. I should have coffee. Have candy. Have a smoke. Don't have a drink. Pills? Hell yes, I would take pills. I search behind the bedstead. I pick through the plush of the bathroom floor mat for any crumb of Kitty's forgotten prescription. What I wouldn't do to find even one tablet with the little chisel: *Watson 932*. It passes the time. If I had a bottleful I would OD. Not in a deliberate attempt to die—I can't plan that far ahead—just to feel the sedation, the deep tide submerge me, because in that instant when I am knocked out there will be real relief. Let whatever happens happen.

There is no chance of getting my job back, but until things can be worked out for them to terminate me free and clear, the Lab does not cancel my health insurance.

* * *

Monday morning, July 22, I begin my days of treatment.

Every morning the sound echoes hollowly off the tiles when I put my coffee cup on the countertop beside the sink. The cup will be there, unwashed, when I get home.

Gradually the cabinets empty of clean cups; gradually a procession of unwashed cups forms beside the sink.

Every weekday a van honks out front and takes me to a rehab program in Española, a double-fenced yard on hardpan, free of tree or sagebrush. Burly orderlies ready to wrestle you to the ground if you get out of hand, a minimum-security prison crossed with a psych ward.

I have a one-on-one intake meeting with a counselor, but the rest of the day it's two-hour sessions where my fellow "clients" go around in a circle, say their first names, and talk about using. Most are Hispanic heroin addicts, many of them on methadone treatment. They talk about *chiva* like a lover, their rhapsodies pure poetry. It's a kind of pornography, hearing them describe how it feels to shoot up behind the McDonald's on Riverside Drive. There are glimpses of redemption, some of them obvious connivances to inflame the enthusiasm of the counselors, who report to the parole officers, who report to the judges.

My turn comes and I say, "Hello, my name is James." They stare at me a long time and wait for me to say more. I stare back. The court order only requires me to show up, sit in the circle, and say my name. They cannot make me say more. I wait.

Every afternoon the van drops one of the other clients in Rinconada. I watch out the window and see the health clinic. I keep an eye out for the blood tech.

At the end of the day I return to the house on Pajarito Road. I no longer call it my house. A letter arrives telling me that I have thirty days to make a payment or the mortgage company will initiate foreclosure proceedings. I have missed just one installment.

Soon this place will belong to the bank and I will have to find somewhere else to sleep—or not sleep, to lie awake at night. I go downstairs to the dining room and check the latch on the slider. When I flip on the outside flood lamps there is nothing there.

I am looking at the procession of empty cups before the van comes to pick me up. The doorbell rings, and a pimpled paralegal from Kitty's lawyer's office serves me divorce papers. I put the papers on the kitchen table and let them sit there. I have thirty days to reply, just like with the mortgage company.

I go to rehab and wait while the time runs out. I don't know how much longer I can take it. I flip on the TV when I get home and there is no more TV. I have not paid the cable bill.

I get permission to leave the house to go to the Mesa Public Library that evening. It's the only card in my wallet that is any good anymore. I check out the memoir *My Country Versus Me*. The thing that bugs me about Wen Ho Lee protesting his mistreatment is how *guilty* he sounds. But somehow he kept it all together. He kept his wife. He kept his house. He kept his money. How?

On August 2, Cahats begins preparing me for the pretrial hearing. "The government is going to look closely at your whole history, even back at your family, when they make their case." I know what's coming. The same shit that's followed me ever since I saw that shrink in college. "Your father spent four years at Fair Oaks in the 1970s."

"Actually, he was in and out intermittently for those four years."

"Why didn't you tell me about this? We can use this in your defense."

"Leave Dad out of it."

"Insanity. It's hereditary, even if it's only temporary. It's the best chance you've got. Beats national-security threat. Trumps attempted terrorism."

If you were the only person in your family who hadn't gone crazy . . .

I catch myself. What if crazy, instead of a 180, is just two clicks away from sane? What if sometimes crazy is right? Like seeing something nobody else sees, and it might be enough? Like Ritchie saying, *Save Church Rock.* Like saying, *Burning lungs . . . burning eyes . . . radiation . . . life expectancy: 12 hours.* But that's crazy. Nothing happened.

No more nightmare, but the memory of the dreams gives rise to another sickness. I brood over the vision: my neighbors in the street, clawing out their own eyes. Nothing is like the living hell of those memories.

I watch my neighbors from the house on Pajarito Road, this house that is not my house: my neighbors in bright shirts driving shiny SUVs to church on Sunday, smiling their constipated smiles. *Purge them by fire . . .* Make it stop. Why doesn't it stop? I delivered the message. *Abandon the community that has forsaken you . . .*

I do not believe in clairvoyance. I know that the drugs, the drink, and sleep deprivation all contributed to the nightmare.

What I do believe in is the house. Meth or no meth, there's something fucked up about that wall. Why was my name up there in the first place? Either someone is playing me like a game or the house itself still has a hold over me. I don't like it either way, but when I last went out there I figured the house would be easier to beat than a personal enemy. I figured wrong.

On Sunday, Kitty comes by to get a few of Oppie's old things. The papers just got filed, but already I cannot look at her like a wife anymore.

"How is your treatment working out?"

"It's not treatment."

"Call it whatever you want."

Sadly, I realize that she is not swearing at me. Kitty has given up that intimacy.

I want to reach out to her, but this would make her hate me even more. I should have kept to my almond cheese and my exercise regimen, but now there is no getting her back.

I love Kitty. I need her. It is futile to suggest otherwise. We could have been nicer to each other. We could have raised a family, even if it meant adoption. We didn't have to be so cruel to each other. I know that she loves me, but she hates me too. And now for her the hate is drowning out the love.

"I miss Oppie," I say. "Do you miss Oppie?"

"Of course I miss Oppie." She already wasn't looking me in the eye, and now she turns away. She won't let me go there. I don't deserve to mourn with her, to mourn like she is mourning. "James, the movers are coming on Tuesday."

"Movers?"

"They said they'd get here early, before you have to leave for your treatment, anyway. All you have to do is let them in. They'll have a list of my stuff and leave you a copy of the manifest . . . What made you start acting so crazy, Jimmy?"

I'm trying to find an answer when she walks away.

Monday after rehab I go by Hank Farmer's and ask to borrow his car.

"I'm not sure I should be letting you do this."

"It's just to get groceries. I'll be back in an hour."

I see her pulling out of the clinic parking lot in a PT Cruiser—cheap, flashy, a car for people who know nothing about cars. I follow her through Chimayó to a trailer on blocks and park across the highway. A ruin of an old adobe sits boarded up beside the trailer. She parks in the shade of an elm that grows out of its crumbling foundation and goes into the trailer.

She emerges half an hour later, alone, having changed out of her scrubs, now transformed into full goth: black blouse and short black skirt, black hair teased into a tufted rat's nest, and torn black stockings.

I follow her into Española. She pulls into the Christian coffee shop.

She orders coffee, sits alone at a booth, and gets on her phone, ghoulish makeup smudged deliberately on her pale skin, a big beauty mark dotting her left cheek.

I sit two booths away with my back to her, listening to snippets of her conversation. "Why don't you go out today, see about that job?" Suddenly I hear her phone snap shut and before I know what's happening the blood tech is standing at my booth, tapping my table with her outrageous nails. "How's your levels?"

My heart leaps into my throat. "Huh?"

"Your cholesterol."

"Not so good."

"James, right? You think you're the only person who can follow people?"

I decide to spit it out. "Been up to Morphy Lake lately?"

"Oh, you know, I've never been to Mora in my life." The way she says it, I know it's true.

"Your friend must have given you some surprise."

"My friend?"

She sees the look in my eyes and settles down opposite me in the booth. Her black stockings are ripped artfully up to her garters. Is this what I gave up Kitty for? Gave up everything?

"Last time you came in for a draw, he was there a few hours before, and he was like, *My friend's turning forty and a bunch of us want to throw him a surprise party*. I said the thing about patient confidentiality and everything and he said, *James O., born on the fourth of July*, and then you came in and it was right there on your chart: *DOB, 7/4/73*."

"What did this guy look like?"

"He was really clean."

"Clean?"

"You know: white, rich, from Los Alamos, like you." The blood tech blushes. "He gave me fifty bucks. I said I didn't want any money. He made me take it anyway."

"Did he say his name?"

"McDonald? McSomething . . ."

The many ways people can manipulate you unless you're aware of the possibilities. I wrote that line.

"Am I in some kind of trouble?" she asks.

"No, you're not in any trouble."

I drive back to Los Alamos and leave Hank's car in his driveway. It's a long walk home down Pajarito Road.

The slider is locked. The crickets are singing. The king-size, springless, formaldehyde-free mattress—I lie on it for the last time. The moving truck is getting here early. I will go out to meet it.

I go down to the dining room in the middle of the night and flip on the light, *plink*. In the glass of the slider I see a man: unshaven, forsaken, tattered, haggard. I cannot look him in the eye, but if he were the subject of one of my profiles I might write: *He has ceased to be troubled by even the most horrifying visions. Disaster, devastation, suffering: he is indifferent before them—unmoved by the misery of man or animal, like nature, but as a man, unnatural. His acquaintances would say they barely recognize him.*

But I recognize him. I flip off the light and make him go away.

I push open the slider, the noise of the door rumbling in its track almost too much to bear. New moon, no moon—crickets going strong on the practice putting green. The crickets in Los Alamos: all these six years I've heard their song, but I never understood the message—mournful, indifferent, a noise beating down on the earth—*you you you you*, and contrapuntal: *real real real real*. Can anybody help me? Where is there someone who hears what I hear? There is no one there.

I shut the slider, sealing myself inside the house like a skeleton in a vault, and pull the curtain to the edge of the glass. I lie on the living room couch and cannot sleep. I am cold but do not move, not even for a blanket. No traffic on Pajarito Road. No distant dog barking.

When the first light of dawn begins glowing against the curtain, the crickets' chorus diminishes—the sound of the world winding down. I rise and stand before the slider, flipping the switch and flooding the room with light. I push aside the curtain to see that ragged man in the glass, and superimposed on him is someone else: handsome in an expensive blue suit.

McCaffery.

"I do not believe that you are here."

"We all come here eventually." I do not open the slider, but I hear him loud and clear.

"The blood tech saw you, though."

"Who says?"

"She says."

"You say she says." He stares back at me through the glass.

I tell him, "I went back to the house."

"You had to warn them."

"I met the old man."

"You had to put the names up on the wall." McCaffery glances eastward at the sky. "It's almost time."

"And if I don't go out to meet it?"

"With or without you, no one will be spared." The light is rising. McCaffery is retreating.

I feel a tremor, hear a sound, and I am lying on the living room couch. The curtain in the dining room is closed.

I open the front door and step over the *Los Alamos Monitor*, registering the date: August 6, Little Boy's birthday, Hiroshima Day.

Hello, my name is James. I am not crazy. I am not afraid to close my eyes.

All across Los Alamos, a thousand Mr. Coffees gurgle on at split-second intervals.

It is a minute past sunrise and it is already hot, a bright summer morning on the Hill. Gracious homes left and right.

Ten thousand people waking up. People with high blood pressure read the paper. People with clean teeth go jogging. People with skin cancer that hasn't been detected yet get ready to go to their jobs.

It is dawn, and Ned, he of the Weedwacker, is already out on his immaculate lawn.

Here I am, barefoot, coming to meet my neighbor between our fields of green. My front lawn is not as nice as Ned's. The grass is shaggy, riddled with dandelions, pocked with old Oppie shits. Ned keeps his lawn close-cropped and free of crabgrass.

"Good morning!"

Ned looks up, waves. He is stringing up his Weedwacker, wearing work boots, eye protection, noise-cancelling headphones.

"Did you hear something?"

He squints at me through the plastic goggles. I make a no-worries gesture. Of course he didn't hear anything. Let me think about this for a second. Was what woke me a sound, or was that just the sound of myself jerking awake?

Ned stoops to yank the cord, once, twice. He is having trouble getting the Weedwacker started. Over Ned's shoulder, down Pajarito Road, the streetlamps are burning in the dawn's early light.

Also available from Akashic Books

HAVANA LUNAR
a Cuban noir novel by Robert Arellano
200 pages, trade paperback original, $14.95
*Finalist for an Edgar Award

"... [T]houghtful, lushly detailed neo-noir ..."
—*Publishers Weekly*

"In this Cuban noir mystery, Arellano engages the reader immediately
by quickly developing his characters into unique individuals, both
good and bad ... Arellano is masterful in weaving both the physical
and the emotional into a story that everyone can relate to in some way,
regardless of geography and politics."
—*MultiCultural Review*

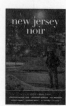

NEW JERSEY NOIR
edited by Joyce Carol Oates
288 pages, trade paperback original, $15.95

Brand-new stories (and poems) by: Joyce Carol Oates, Robert Arellano,
Jonathan Safran Foer, Robert Pinsky, S.J. Rozan, Edmund White &
Michael Carroll, Bradford Morrow, Sheila Kohler, S.A. Solomon, Jeffrey
Ford, Jonathan Santlofer, Gerald Stern, and others.

"Oates's introduction to Akashic's noir volume dedicated to the
Garden State, with its evocative definition of the genre, is alone with
the price of the book."
—*Publishers Weekly*

DON DIMAIO OF LA PLATA
a novel by Robert Arellano
208 pages, trade paperback original, $13.95

"A former student of Robert Coover, Arellano has created a brilliant
novel of political satire based on an actual mayoral stint in Providence,
RI ... Recommended for all fiction collections."
—*Library Journal*

"Robert Arellano's new book is one of the bawdiest, dirtiest, rowdiest,
and raunchiest novels I've come across in a long time. And it's hilarious.
Hurling words like tainted pitchforks, he pursues his wanton prey as
if on speed himself, snort by snort, sexual escapade by sexual escapade,
as Don Dimaio lays waste to the city he's supposed to govern ... Don
Dimaio is an antihero for all ages, or for any adolescent/postadolescent
in heat and in love with language."
—*Providence Sunday Journal*

FAST EDDIE, KING OF THE BEES
a novel by Robert Arellano
240 pages, trade paperback original, $14.95

"The story of Oedipus underlies Arellano's first 'print' novel, but the main story here is the author's style, which takes its cue from William S. Burroughs, Philip K. Dick, Charles Dickens, Jack Kerouac, and Tom Robbins. This may be the first postapocalyptic novel in which the apocalypse was created by a public works project, Boston's Big Dig . . . [a] funny and surprising book. Recommended for literary collections."
—*Library Journal*

RUINS
a novel by Achy Obejas
208 pages, trade paperback original, $15.95
*A selection of the Barnes & Noble Discover Great New Writers program

"[P]rize-winning, ever-innovative Cuban American writer Obejas evinces a new, focused lyricism as she penetrates to the very heart of the Cuban paradox in a story as pared down and intense as its narrator's life."
—*Booklist*

THE SWING VOTER OF STATEN ISLAND
a novel by Arthur Nersesian
272 pages, trade paperback, $15.95
*Book one of The Five Books of Moses series

"Nersesian's extravagantly imagined dystopia relies—as did those of Philip Roth's *Plot Against America* and Michael Chabon's *Yiddish Policemen's Union*—on an alternate, counterfactual history."
—*New York Times Book Review*

"A rousing, intricately detailed romp that eschews laments over a long-gone 'old New York' in favor of a speculative paean to Gotham's unparalleled mutability."
—*Time Out New York*